A Place of Filtered Sunshine

A Place of Filtered Sunshine

~

Kelly Kathryn Griffin

Kelly Kathryn Griffin

Writers Club Press
San Jose New York Lincoln Shanghai

A Place of Filtered Sunshine

All Rights Reserved © 2001 by Kelly Kathryn Griffin

No part of this book may be reproduced or transmitted in any form or by any means, graphic, electronic, or mechanical, including photocopying, recording, taping, or by any information storage retrieval system, without the permission in writing from the publisher.

Writers Club Press
an imprint of iUniverse.com, Inc.

For information address:
iUniverse.com, Inc.
5220 S 16th, Ste. 200
Lincoln, NE 68512
www.iuniverse.com

This is a work of fiction. Although inspired by actual events, places, and historical persons, the names, activities, and characters of the town of Blanc Fleur are inventions of the author. Any resemblance to people living or deceased is purely coincidental.

ISBN: 0-595-18082-5

Printed in the United States of America

For Mom and Dad

Acknowledgements

Thank you to Eileen Lawson for editing my book. Danke to John Griffin for supplying the German words.

Chapter 1

Nettie pulled her coat tighter around her to keep out the May chill. This motion caused the letter tucked carefully in her breast pocket to rustle. She reached into her coat and pulled out the long, crisp envelope and stared at it. It was addressed to her, "Mademoiselle Bernadette Dupre, Village of Blanc Fleur, Normandy, France." Her interest was drawn to the return address, which simply stated, "R. Wieber, Koln, Germany." The words seemed simple but the accompanying emotions were anything but.

She was startled as a small child threw her arms around her waist and said "Thanks for bringing us, Aunt Nettie, we are having such fun!" She quietly put the letter back into her pocket and leaned down to hug her niece. "Well, I love bringing you here, and I'm glad we were able to come before the anniversary."

"What's an anni...anniver...," stammered seven year old Simone.

"Anniversary," finished her Aunt.

"Yea, that."

"It's sort of a birthday for an event rather than a person," explained her Aunt. "In a few weeks it will be the 15th anniversary of the Allied..." A confused look from her niece caused her to hasten, "of the American,

British, and Canadian soldiers to cross that channel and land on this very beach, Omaha Beach."

"Were you here when they landed?" Simone inquired.

"Yes…not on the beach of course!" she quickly added. "I was in town with your grandmother and great-grandmother." A dark shadow crossed the older woman's face as they turned and walked along the cliffs in silence. It was after they walked down a steep ravine and up the other side that Nettie realized that they had come to an area that she had avoided for years, sixteen years to be exact.

"I'm hungry. Can we go now?" piped up Simone.

"Yes, go find your brother and sisters and we will go home," agreed her aunt.

Simone raced off to find twelve year old Michel and Marie and Terese, who were ten and five respectively.

Nettie looked around where she stood. Yes, the large boulder was still perched perilously on the cliff and a soft mound of earth that rose nearly as high as the boulder was still situated about ten feet away from that rock. Nettie took a seat on the cold, hard boulder and looked out over the channel. The water was a cloudy gray, like the color of his eyes, she mused. It had been so long since she had thought of him—no, that wasn't true. In some way he was always in the back of her mind. She closed her eyes and placed her hand over the letter and pressed it to her heart. Her ears filled with the pounding surf and calling of the gulls. The years began to melt away and she could just about see him sitting before her on the soft earth and…

"We're ready!" shouted Teresa. "Are you OK, Aunt Nettie?" For such a young girl she was able to catch the change in mood in her aunt.

"I'm fine," she managed to smile "but we need to get home. Do we have everything? Michel, shake out the blankets before we get into the car please. Now where did we park the car?"

They finally located their car on a back dirt road. She had parked there even though the roads in and around the cliffs were mostly paved now. Parking lots had been built to hold the cars of the visitors to the beaches and to the cemeteries. But Nettie rarely visited the areas patronized by the scores of tourists who visited the site of the Allied invasion on June 6th, 1944. She occasionally visited the cemetery that held the bodies of the Allied forces and stood in awe of the row upon row of white crosses and Stars of David that seemed to go on forever. She had never visited the cemetery containing the German soldiers; she already knew it did not hold the body of a certain young man that the war had devoured. When she did visit the cliffs she stayed off the beaten paths. She tried to remember the area as it was when she was a child and walked the beaches with her father and believed it was "her beach". Now the once-personal haven belonged to the world and had the strange name of a tribe of people half a world away. As she drove down the main road home, passing the last of the tourist cars and buses heading to the site for the day, her mind wandered back to the time when the roads were muddy and rutted and the occupying forces fenced off and mined their beaches. The children's chatter about the afternoon barely distracted Nettie's thoughts of the past.

It was only a few moments before they came to the low stone fence that encircled the Dupre apple orchard. She ignored the sign that pointed visitors to the "Dupre Distillery and Orchard" to park across the street from the white farmhouse and pulled into the driveway adjoining the house. The children piled out of the car and with called "thanks" and "bye's", they ran off down the path to their home located at the back of the orchard. She looked down the dirt road to the distillery and saw her brother deep in conversation with a group of people, all with cameras draped over their shoulders. "Tourists," she figured and called to Pierre, her brother, to let him know that his children were home. He raised his dark head and waved a greeting. For a moment she stood looking at him. The letter brought back the memories of those years ago when she was so angry with her brother and never wanted to see him again, and yet she had feared just that.

She entered the side door that led into the kitchen and found that dinner was on the stove. Her mother was setting the table for the two of them when she glanced up and said, "That was good timing. Go get cleaned up and then we can eat." She looked at her daughter and noticed the rather odd expression etched on her face. "Are you OK, Nett? They weren't too much trouble were they?"

"Oh no," she assured her mother. After a pause she said "I got a letter today. It's from Rolfe."

Her mother did a double take and managed to stammer, "What does it say, Nett?"

"I haven't read it yet. Can I have a few minutes to myself to read it before dinner?"

"Of course, dinner will keep. Take all the time you need."

Nettie shrugged off her coat and left it on a kitchen chair before she climbed the stairs to the second floor. At the top she hesitated. She had become momentarily confused, seeing the second floor as it had been fifteen years ago. Her brother's room had been to the left, and down the narrow hallway to the right, you would find, in order, her and Terese's room, a tiny bathroom, and at the end of the hall, her mother's room. She shook her head as if to clear the past and looked again to see the second floor as it now was. The large landing doubled as a day room with a loveseat and overstuffed chair. A door led to Nettie's private bedroom and bath. It was much smaller than the original floor that had been destroyed by a crashing airplane in the first day of the invasion of Normandy. Money had been scarce after the war and it was years before they could afford to rebuild. By that time Nana had died, her brother had built his own small home and with her mother living downstairs in Nana's old room, the space would only have to house Nettie. Yes, only Nettie, since Terese would not be coming home. With the thought of her much younger sister, Nettie sighed and looked again at the letter in her hand. Perhaps it would be better left unread, best left in the past, those bitter memories of long ago. She stepped into her room and closed the door behind her.

She sat on the end of her bed and, holding her breath, broke the seal of the envelope and pulled out several neatly folded sheets of paper. She wanted to toss them in the trashcan next to her dresser, but she glanced at the handwriting. Yes, she recognized the way the words were put to paper. The bold capital letters, the precise pinpoints over the 'i's. She lifted the paper closer to her eyes and was startled to discover that they contained a slight spicy musk scent that she had not come across since in those fifteen years. With the pages brought up to her nose she breathed deeply again and exhaled. She unfolded the pages and began a journey back to a summer day in 1943.

Chapter 2

Nettie stood in front of the old beveled mirror and ran the brush through her long, dark hair with tired, impatient strokes. Her thin face was drawn with worry and her eyes sunken.

"Nettie, are you coming down for breakfast?" It was her mother calling from the bottom of the stairs. Her forced chipper call wasn't successful in blocking out a concerned overtone to her simple question.

"Yes," she shouted back. She braided the strands of hair into one thick rope, tied it off and threw it over her shoulder. She looked at her reflection and, knowing it would not do to show such a face to her mother and grandmother, pinched her cheeks to redden them and forced a smile and spring in her step and then headed for the stairs.

After a simple breakfast of toast with apple butter accompanied by forced idle chatter, Nettie made a hurried escape from the farmhouse and headed to the stone garage. Inside leaned her bicycle. She kicked up the stand and turned it around to head out down the driveway and into the road. To her surprise she found her grandmother, or Nana, as she was called, standing at the entrance of the garage.

"Don't worry, Nett. The pass should be here any day now. In a few days you'll be drinking tea with your Great Aunt Colette and all this will be behind you."

Her granddaughter shook her head sadly. "Nana, they'll never let me go. It doesn't matter anyway, I hear things aren't much better in Vichy." Nana laid a work-callused hand on Nettie's arm. "My friend knows someone who can be bribed and we are just waiting for the final instructions and then you'll be on your way."

"Who is your friend Nana? You don't even know to whom you are giving your money, do you?"

Her grandmother merely answered, "It's all arranged, Nett. You'll be on your way in a week, I promise."

Nettie mounted her bicycle and pedaled down the drive, calling over her shoulder, "I'll see you tonight." She pedaled her bicycle over the rutted road faster than one should, but then again what did she have to lose?

She was out of breath when she came within 50 yards of the town gate. With a sudden idea she turned down a narrow road to her right and traveled a quarter mile down it to the end. A neatly lettered sign indicated that it was the "Cemetery of St. Mary's Catholic Church." Dismounting, she leaned the bicycle against the iron fence and pushed open the gate. The cemetery adjoining the church had filled up ages ago and this ground held the departed of the last half-century or so. She plucked a few blooms of the wild flowers that had cropped up here and there and made her way to a small area outlined in bricks near the center of the cemetery. She read the headstones and placed a flower at each head stone as she strolled by. The first was of Jacques Ratisseau, 1849-1925, her mother's father and Nana's husband. The second was of Guillaume Dupre, 1885-1934, her father. The last stone was smaller than the others were and the shape of a lamb was engraved at the top. She leaned over and pulled the intrusive grass away from the face of the stone. The words simply stated, 'Our Lamb, Guillaume Dupre, 1909-1918,' her older brother. It was on his grave she sat down on the still moist grass and absent-mindedly plucked the petals off the last flower she held. She raised her head and through the bars of the fence that surrounded the cemetery found she had a clear view of the town of Blanc Fleur. A twenty-foot stone wall and impressive iron gate guarded the northern face of the town. However, apparently the town's leaders realized that the town was not strategically located over a river, a port, or, in fact, anything of importance, and the other three walls were never completed. In the Middle Ages as now, the true wealth of the town lay in the farmers' fields that were full of grain, livestock, or as in the Dupre's case, apples.

Nettie stood back up and shook out her long navy serge skirt and walked over to the fence and surveyed the top of the wall. German soldiers leaned against the thick walls, a few drinking out of tin cups, a few smoking, and she noticed one was looking back at her through field glasses. A feeling of disgust rose in her stomach; was there no getting away from them? Just then the church bells rang the three-quarters hour and she realized she must hurry to get to the school on time.

She pedaled quickly down the narrow lane and headed directly through the city gates. A few German soldiers waved her through without her stopping. She was forced to slow down on the old cobblestones that lined the village streets. The workday had already started for the inhabitants and people were out and about on their daily business. Intermingled with the citizens were German soldiers and other foreign nationals that worked at various levels of willingness for the Third Reich. Very few of these interlopers actually lived in Blanc Fleur; most were on leave from their duties on the cliffs over-looking the Channel, which was less than five miles up the road that passed the Dupre orchard. Nettie eyed groups of people in the midst of animated conversations. Was she imagining it or was there a certain buzz in the air? She kept riding up the main street, passing the gate of the school, and saw that several of her colleagues were standing and talking on the school steps. A block further up the street she pulled onto a small path next to the public library. Dismounting, she pushed open the large privacy gate that led to a garden behind the library. She leaned her bicycle against the ancient Gothic wall that had once housed an ancient church. It was said that they were so thick that cannon balls would bounce right off them. Of course they hoped never to find that out, but they had certainly held up during the centuries that had seen famine, plagues and several conquests, including the latest one.

The Germans had come during the summer of 1940 after meeting little in the way of resistance. France had found itself woefully unprepared in the face of Germany's Wehrmacht (war machine), and the fight was a short one. Insidiously, the Third Reich, as they called their "New World," had taken over every aspect of the villagers' lives. Travel was all but suspended; curfews were in effect from dusk to dawn and ration coupons must be used to purchase everything from gasoline to sugar. Nana had once commented that she was surprised that they hadn't handed out coupons for prayers in church. Nettie had dryly answered that the war wasn't over yet.

Nettie pushed open the heavy wooden entry door to the library and waved at Lily, the librarian. Lily was busy straightening the circulation desk, so she merely returned the wave to her friend. Nettie knew that Lily appreciated the use of her bicycle to run errands and Nettie in turn needed a safe, out-of-the-way place to park her bicycle. Lily had had her own bicycle at one time. It was still fresh in everyone's mind that day last year when Lily had made the mistake of parking her bicycle in front of the library. Hauptmann Neuman, the Commandant of Blanc Fleur, drunk as usual, had taken the wheel of his Mercedes and run over Lily's bicycle. The sight that followed was one that Nettie and the other townspeople would not forget. The Commandant had jumped out of his vehicle and was screaming about the scratches on his car and that someone was going to pay for the damages. About that time Lily came out of the library and was matching curse word for curse word with the Commandant. People had begun to scatter for cover when Frederick, the Commandant's aide and the usual driver of the car, ran up the street and stood between the two feuding parties. In a calm voice he talked the Commandant into getting into the passenger seat while he took the wheel and drove back to Headquarters. Later it was rumored that the Commandant had been so drunk that he didn't remember the incident. Nettie herself didn't think he had been *that* drunk, but believed that he might have had help getting *that* drunk after he reached his office. She did know that Frederick had arranged for the scratches on the Mercedes to be repaired quickly.

After closing the library door, Nettie hurried down the street and passed through the tall, wrought iron gates leading to the courtyard that was lined by three buildings. The two-story brick building to the right was the German Headquarters of Blanc Fleur and the surrounding areas. Before the war it had held the classrooms of the upper grades. Directly in front of her was a one-story building that once was the school gymnasium and lunchroom. Now it served as the general barracks for German soldiers. To her left was a two-story brick building that was a twin to the one directly opposite. It used to house the lower grades and now it swelled with the upper grades that were housed there as well.

The clock tower struck 8a.m. as Nettie approached the school's stoop. Children made mad rushes into the entrances of the building so as to not be late for school. She greeted her fellow teachers that had not moved inside and stood as if waiting for her.

Nettie laughed at a middle-aged man as he spit out a cigarette he was smoking with obvious distaste. "Francois, *what* are you smoking now?" she asked.

"Corn silk, and it's just not the same," he answered with disgust. The whole group burst into raucous laughter. They were well versed in his attempts to find an acceptable substitute for the hard-to-find and expensive tobacco.

"Hi Nett," greeted Clea, the first grade teacher. This morning her blonde hair was attractively done up in a twist and extra care had been taken in applying her make-up. The gray suit she wore was the best she owned.

"Clea, you look like the cat's meow this morning, what gives?" questioned Nettie.

"You will never guess who arrived last night…the new Commandant!" Clea breathlessly answered her own question.

"How do you know?" asked Nettie, blanching.

"His motorcade stopped across from my house late last night. He is staying at the Cohen house."

"I don't think the Cohens will be back," broke in Francois, "and if the Germans had their way *I* wouldn't be here either!"

"Francois, please don't wave your hands around like that," begged Margarethe.

"Oh don't worry! Remember that I am a happily married man!"

"Yes, and how is the missus?" quizzed Anna.

"She is wonderful, what a peach! She takes care of the house and cats and I take care of the garden and the cooking. If she were a man I would kiss her!"

"Francois!" scolded Margarethe. The rest of the group burst into renewed merriment. They were so involved in their conversation they did not notice a small group of soldiers approaching them.

"Guten Morgen, ladies and gentlemen, I trust your young scholars are not as rambunctious as their teachers!" hailed the well-dressed German soldier closest to them.

"It's the Commandant," hissed Clea under her breath, stating the fact they had already guessed.

"We are so sorry Herr Commandant," spoke up Anna. "We are never this loud; I am so sorry, Herr Commandant! It will never happen again Herr Commandant!"

He looked rather surprised at this outburst and stepped back as if expecting her to fall on his well-polished boots at any moment. "That's fine, just fine," he answered. His visor on his cap hid his eyes, but they could tell he was looking over their little group: the attractive blonde at the top of the stairs, the effeminate middle-aged man standing near the railing on a middle stair, next to him the redheaded young woman who had answered him and at the bottom of the stairs a woman with a long dark braid running down her back, her eyes cast downward, and an older woman with thick glasses desperately trying to hide behind the younger one's thin form.

"I will leave you to your young scholars then. Have a pleasant, and I hope, quiet day." He tipped his cap and turned to walk across the courtyard to what would be his new Headquarters.

Nettie glanced up when she heard him say goodbye and gasped inwardly when she caught his eyes resting oh so briefly on her. She was relieved when no one noticed her slight jump. They stood there in stunned silence until Margarethe spoke up. "Whew! We must be more careful."

"Isn't he gorgeous?" Gushed Clea: "I mean tall, blonde…"

"Armed and dangerous, my god! I'm in love," laughed Francois in a fake swoon. "Really Clea! What are you thinking? Well, I am sure the youth of France are breathlessly awaiting their results of their algebra exam." And with that he walked up the steps and entered the school.

"Oh brother!" huffed Clea as the remainder of the group headed for their respective classrooms.

Nettie, suddenly feeling ill, held onto the bannister while she climbed the stairs to the second floor. Only a few doors down she came to her fourth-grade classroom and opened the door. Not to her surprise, she found that Sister Marie-Claire was already there taking the roll and inquiring about a sick classmate. Her serge habit covered everything but her kind face and her hands that were always in motion, and occasionally, a stray wisp of dark blonde hair. Marie-Claire loved the children and it showed in her hugs and the way she nurtured their hearts while Nettie tried to nurture their minds. Usually the 22 students were well behaved, but the stress and hardship of the last three years had left the children anxious and angry at times. After a smile and a nod to Marie-Claire, Nettie gathered her group of students in front of the blackboard and had them practice their math problems. In the back of the room, Marie-Claire sat on the floor and was trying to teach spelling. As usual, most of the children were either on her lap or hanging onto one of her limbs.

The morning was progressing smoothly and Nettie had almost managed to push the memory of the meeting with the new Commandant from her mind when a knock came at the door. Nettie, not having a child hanging on her at that moment, crossed the room and opened the door. She found Frederick, the tall, redheaded aide to the Commandant, standing there with a German soldier she did not recognize.

"Please come with us, Fraulein Dupre," answered Frederick to Nettie's inquiry of how she could help them. "The new Commandant would like to speak to you." His eyes gave nothing away as she looked at him hoping to catch a clue as to what this summons meant. She turned and mouthed to Marie-Claire that she would return when she was done. Marie-Claire forced a smile and nod for the sake of the watching children. Nettie followed her escorts down the main staircase, down the front stairs, and across the courtyard. They entered the twin of the building of that they had just left and instead of turning left to where Commandant Neumann had kept his office, they continued up the main staircase and turned left. Down a few doors they stopped before a door that Nettie had entered before.

Chapter 3

A crisp "Enter" was given as a response to Frederick's knock on the door. Nettie was ushered into the room and the soldiers turned on their heels and left the room, shutting the door behind them. Fear gripped her as she stood staring at the closed door through which the soldiers had just retreated. She stood at the back of what used to be a classroom—her classroom, in fact. The walls that had once held the classics that she had taught and posters of the various countries represented in those stories were all gone. In their places were maps of Europe with various pins sticking in them. Posters of Hitler exhalting the Third Reich seemed to take up most of the wall space. Toward the front of the classroom where her modest metal desk had stood was an enormous carved wooden desk. Seated behind the desk was the Commandant. She had been so intent on looking at her old classroom that the fear had subsided, but in an instant the fear arose again and she could barely catch her breath. She looked at the man behind the desk and dropped her eyes, seemly finding her shoes ever so fascinating.

"Please, have a seat," spoke the Commandant in French. Slowly Nettie lifted her eyes to find the Commandant looking at her. She was rather surprised to find that while his eyes were a rather intense gray, they were not unkind. She found some courage and closed the gap between them and took a seat in a wooden chair on the opposite side of the enormous desk. She sat stiffly as she said, "Danke, Herr Commandant."

"Sprechen sie Deutch?" he asked with some surprise.

"Ja, mein Vater ist aus Alsace gekommen."

"You are German?"

"No, I am French," Nettie answered firmly in French.

He brought the cigarette he was smoking to his lips and watched as the smoke blew out of his mouth. Nettie could smell the rich aroma of tobacco, not one of the cheap imitations that Francois and several others were forced to smoke.

He continued, "I thank you for interrupting your busy schedule. I recognize you from this morning as one of the teachers."

Nettie merely nodded in the affirmative. Beneath her eyelashes she looked at his sun-bleached hair and lined face as he dragged deeply again on his cigarette, his eyes closing as he enjoyed the moment. Even his eyelashes appeared white. With a start she realized that he had opened his eyes and was looking at her.

"Were you in North Africa?" she heard herself ask.

"What makes you say that?" he inquired.

"You ah…" she stammered, suddenly feeling both foolish and afraid that she had asked a personal question of the Commandant. "You look so…bleached," she finished in a voice barely above a whisper.

"Yes, actually I was. I was under Rommel's command until I received this post. I learned some French while I was in North Africa, which has helped considerably. Anything else you want to know?" he replied in a rather casual, off-handed manner. She had several things she wanted to ask this man, but she knew better than to ask him any more questions. "No, Hauptmann…. I'm sorry, I do not know your name."

"First, my name is Wieber, Rolfe Wieber. Second, I am not Hauptmann Wieber, my rank is Oberleutnant. But I would prefer to be called Commandant Wieber as that refers to my position here at Blanc Fleur rather than my rank in the army. Would you please tell that to your colleagues and friends, Fraulein Dupre?"

"Yes, Herr Commandant." She looked at her shoes again.

"Are you surprised they would assign a lowly Oberleutnant to Blanc Fleur?"

"Oh no, Commandant. It's just that nothing really happens here anyway."

"Really?" he asked rather sarcastically. Nettie didn't reply and her eyes returned to staring at the floor.

After a moment of silence the Commandant spoke up. "I asked you to come to see me because I understand you were present when my predecessor died." With that statement he snuffed out his cigarette in an already overflowing ashtray. "In fact, I understand he died on your farm."

While Nettie expected the question, she nonetheless had to grip the arms of the chair to steady her. She took a deep breath and chose her words carefully. "I keep bees and I sell the honey." After hesitating she continued, "He wanted to get a closer look at the hive. I told him it was not safe, but he got too close, tripped, and fell onto one of the hives." She stopped again, trying to act distraught over the loss of that evil animal masquerading as a human being. "He was stung hundreds of times and they think he was allergic to them."

He looked harder at her. "Is that all?" he asked.

"Yes. Frederick was there, surely he told you what happened." Her voice trailed off as she gripped harder at the arms of the chair in which she was seated. Surely the interrogations were over.

"Ja, he told me the same story, and of course I have been over the reports, but I like to ask my own questions."

"Of course," she murmured softly, her eyes still fixed to the floor.

"I also understand that you wish to travel to Vichy to visit a relative."

"My great aunt is ill and I am needed to care for her."

"I am sorry to report that I must deny the request on the grounds of your history. Perhaps at a later date," he offered.

A deafening silence followed, broken only by the sounds of the Commandant shifting in his chair.

"So, what do you teach?" he asked as he sat up and put his elbows on the desk. "What subjects?"

"Fourth grade," she replied "but I used to teach literature to the older students."

"You must have had this room."

Nettie's face showed honest surprise. "How did you know?"

"For someone called in to see the Commandant you seemed more interested in the room, but then again you already knew what I was going to ask you, didn't you?" He didn't wait for an answer but went on, "I don't suppose this was your desk?"

Nettie found herself smiling at the thought. "No, this was downstairs in the Commandant's office. I think it originally came from the bank."

"What classroom is yours now?" He motioned toward the building across the courtyard.

"Or is it on the other side?"

"It's that one." She motioned with her head to the room straight across from where they were sitting. "I share the teaching duties with Sister Marie-Claire."

He straightened up. "I am sure she is wondering where you are. Thank you for coming to see me." He got to his feet and Nettie followed suit. He came around to her side of the desk and escorted her to the door and opened it. "I trust you can find your own way back to your classroom."

Nettie hoped she didn't look too relieved to be leaving his company as she brushed by him to leave the room. She had to hold herself back to prevent herself from sprinting down the staircase. At the bottom of the stairs Frederick, who just happened to be heading out the door at the same time, joined her.

"How did it go?" the tall German asked out of the side of his mouth.

Without looking at him, Nettie answered, "He asked about what happened to Commandant Neumann. What did he do, ask about me the minute he got to his new office this morning?"

Frederick looked uncomfortable as he answered. "That's the odd thing. He seemed to know everything before he even got here. Of course, he probably asked why the position was open."

Without another word Frederick headed to the barracks and Nettie continued on across the courtyard and up the stairs to her classroom.

Nettie opened the door to find several children in tears, which magically disappeared when they saw her enter the room. Several came to throw their arms around her.

"Good heavens! Such a fuss!" she tried to say in an upbeat manner. But in truth her heart was just now slowing down. She understood that several of the children had witnessed other knocks on the door and someone being led off, never to be seen again or else come back, changed in ways they couldn't understand at their age. Marie-Claire flashed her a relieved smile from where she stood at the front of the room.

That afternoon darkened with a coming storm. The lights were turned on in most of the rooms in the buildings overlooking the courtyard. This allowed the activity of each building to be observed by persons in the buildings opposite. Normally, Nettie didn't bother to look across the courtyard to see what the Germans were up to, but today she found herself sneaking looks across the square on several occasions. Once, while writing on the blackboard, she felt the hair on her neck stand up. She glanced over her shoulder and saw a figure standing at the window directly opposite her. She knew instinctively who it was and she slowly turned her face back toward the blackboard and composed herself before steadying her hand and continuing to write the assignments for the up-coming weekend.

It was after the three o'clock bell rang for dismissal and the students had gathered up their belongings and marched out of the classroom before Nettie could talk privately to Marie-Claire. The nun lent a sympathetic ear as Nettie told her all that had happened in the Commandant's office and that her request to go to Vichy had been denied.

She was exhausted as she left the school and made her way up the street to the library to retrieve her bicycle. She was grateful that the rain had stopped, she wanted to get home as quickly as possible. She opened the gate and found her bicycle leaning up against the wall.

"Oh damn!" she muttered under her breath as she noticed a soggy red ribbon tied to her bicycle basket. She took the ribbon off and stuffed it into her skirt pocket and led her bicycle to the street. After she mounted she had to ride slowly on the slippery cobblestones to avoid running over the milling villagers and soldiers. As she pedaled to the gate that led to the road home she noticed a small group of soldiers standing near the entrance. She wouldn't have even paid any attention to them but one waved at her and seemed to be ordering her to stop. She had skidded to a stop on the cobblestones before she realized that it was the Commandant.

"Fraulen Dupre, we meet again," he greeted her. "Please let me drive you home, it's too muddy to ride home on a bicycle."

As if she wanted his company! "Danke, Commandant Wieber, but I couldn't trouble you to take so much of your time out of your schedule, but I do thank you." With that she pedaled as fast as she dared to put as much distance between them as she could. The thought of being in the same car with him terrified her. She also wondered how he knew what road she took home.

Three years of military trucks and tanks had made the road a mess. It was even worse after it rained as it had that day. However, after the day she had had, she barely noticed the mud caked to her bicycle and clothing. Finally, the two-story farmhouse came into view and at the break in the low stone wall she pedaled into the garage and parked her bicycle. She pulled off her shoes and left them on the steps leading to the side door and stepped into the kitchen. She breathed deeply of the aroma wafting from the oven. Her Grandmother Ratisseau, Nana to her family, was stirring something on the stove.

"Ah, there you are, we were getting worried. Your mother is getting cleaned up and it looks like you need to too," she finished with nary a breath between sentences.

She found her mother washing up in the upstairs bathroom. Her mother looked weary. While Nettie worked at school, Nana worked around the house, took care of the chickens, and did the cooking. Her daughter, Nettie's mother, took care of the garden and the orchard. Granted, Nana and Nettie helped when they could, but most of the physical labors rested on her slender shoulders. They had decided that if they had a future after the war the orchard must be kept in some kind of order. But after three years the question of what that future might be had crossed more than one mind.

As they washed the mud from their limbs, Nettie told her mother about the new Commandant and the meeting in his office that morning. "He said that my pass to Vichy was denied. I hope you can get your money back, mother. It was a nice idea, but I didn't really think they would just let me ride out of Blanc Fleur that easily. Besides, Vichy is collaborating with the Germans. I doubt anyone there would help me."

"Don't worry Nett, I hadn't paid a dime for the papers. I guess I can tell you now that I had planned to have you smuggled to Spain from Vichy. For a price you can find someone to do anything." Her mother left her concern for her daughter unspoken. Strange, the new Commandant had just arrived last night and obviously was already interested in her whereabouts.

As if to lighten the conversation, her mother commented, "So he has already set up his office in your old classroom. Well, at least you won't get lost the next time he sends for you." She had meant it to be a joke, but when she noticed her daughter had stopped washing and was looking at her with tears welling up in her eyes, she held her daughter's face in her hands, leaned in and said, "You need to put it out of your mind. It's over; no one is going to find out anything. They didn't find out anything in June and that new Commandant won't find out anything now."

"But momma," she grasped her mother's hands, "they don't need to *prove* anything. All they need to do is knock on our door and take me away. All that man needs is a feeling that something isn't right and I am gone." Her mother hugged her close. She had no idea what else she could do for her daughter, since she knew what she said was true.

At dinner they tried to keep the chatter light. "Oh yes, I nearly forgot," Nettie said as she reached into the pocket of the work pants she had changed into and pulled out the red ribbon she had taken from her bicycle. "I guess there goes my nice quiet weekend." Yes, agreed her mother, but perhaps it would give her something to think about.

As darkness fell, Nettie went to sit on the swing on the front porch. Her mother had retired to her room upstairs and Nana had gone to bed in her room off the kitchen. It was a rare moment that she had peace and quiet. It seemed her whole life was taken up by demanding children and the never-ending chores around the house and orchard. The early August evening was wonderfully mild, with a slight breeze coming off from the not-too-distant ocean. She breathed deeply of its cool goodness and listened contentedly to the sounds of insects creating a chorus of sounds in the trees and grass. Every once in a while a rustle in a bush would quiet the nocturnal chant, but after a few moments of expectant silence, the sounds would reverberate again.

Her eyes were adjusted to the darkness and her ears to the sounds of the night when she stood up and made her way off the porch. She listened for any hint of activity on the road that ran by her house. It ran from the village, picked up traffic from a road leading to the nearby town of Bayeux and ended at the cliffs. It was usually a bevy of activity with a steady stream of military and farm vehicles going back and forth. Tonight it was unusually quiet on the muddy and rutted road.

 The moon had risen high in the sky and offered plenty of light to Nettie as she made her way around the side of the house and started on the path that led through the apple orchard. For nearly two hundred yards she made her way through the fruit laden trees. She paused at the edge of the clearing, listening carefully. In front of her were a series of wells and cisterns, their forms rising eerily up in the moonlight. They were laid out in two long rows, intersecting near the center of each. She cautiously made her way to a cistern on one of the ends and took off its wooden cover and laid it aside. Instead of seeing water, she saw the wooden plug that prevented anything from dropping more than three feet. She looked inside and with the light of the moon could make out the shape of a package that had been left inside. She lifted it out and gently placed it on the ground while she replaced the wooden cover. She picked the object back up and discovered it had been wrapped in a burlap bag. After hesitating one last time to listen to the night sounds around her, she quietly made her way back to the path and toward the farmhouse. Where the trees stopped at the yard of the farmhouse, Nettie left the path and followed the tree line to a small workman's shed tucked just into the orchard and out of sight of the house. She unlocked the door with one hand and entered, closing the door behind her. Setting the package on a workbench, she fumbled for a box of matches she knew to be there and, finding them, struck one. She quickly lit the waiting kerosene lamp also set on the workbench. She turned the flame down; she didn't want to attract any attention from anyone who may be wandering around this time of night, especially those of the German persuasion. She grasped a crowbar hanging on the wall and knelt down before the workbench. Quietly as possible, she pried up a board and revealed a small crawl space. She stood up and gently picked the burlap wrapped package and placed it into the crawl space and replaced the board. Extinguishing the flame, she left the building, locking the door behind her. Without turning on a light, she entered the farmhouse via the side door and silently made her way through the kitchen and up the stairs.

After undressing in the dark, she pulled the cotton nightgown over her head and crawled into bed. She lay there, unable to sleep, her mind replaying the stressful encounters with the new Commandant. In her mind she mulled over her options. Perhaps she could slip out of town without the Commandant's knowledge. No, that wouldn't work. While she herself might be able to escape, what about her mother and Nana? Nothing could protect them from his expected wrath and she doubted if Nana could handle such a strenuous ordeal. Feeling rather defeated, Nettie sighed and turned over and after a few moments fell into a deep sleep.

Chapter 4

The next day being Saturday offered no respite from the daily grind of work. After an early breakfast, Nana went to feed the chickens and clean the coop. Nettie's mother went out to her never-ending chores in the orchard and Nettie herself headed for the old workman's shack. After opening the windows to let in some light and fresh air and drawing the gauze curtains to prevent anyone passing by on the road to see inside, Nettie locked the door. She pried up the floorboard covering the crawl space. The package, as expected, was still there and she reached down and picked it up and set it on the workbench. The burlap bag was tied off with a piece of twine and Nettie had to fumble through the tools laying scattered about to find a pair of scissors with which to cut the twine. When she took the object out of the sack, she was amazed. Not for what it was, a radio, but what a fine radio it was. It was made out of silver and mahogany, and she could tell the workmanship was of the finest quality. She wondered which of her neighbors could afford such a beautiful piece. She shrugged; maybe someone from a nearby village had heard of her radio repair service. Usually a note was included to indicate what was wrong with the item, but after searching the sack and looking over the radio she came up empty handed.

She next laid out an assortment of screwdrivers and pliers on the workbench and reached up and placed her finger in a small indentation in the tool-covered wall. It slid back easily and revealed a three-foot by three-foot shallow cabinet. On various narrow shelves rested radio tubes, wires, and other spare radio parts. She really doubted if she had anything that would fit into this obviously one-of-a-kind radio. She gently took the back off the radio and looked inside. She was rather relieved to see several wires that appeared to be disconnected or loose. She carefully reached in with a screwdriver and tightened the wires and then made sure all of the tubes fit snuggly in their sockets. With a deep breath she plugged in the radio and turned an engraved silver knob. To her great relief a faint strain of music greeted her ears. The sound quality was wonderful; not that she was surprised. She missed not listening to the radio. Ah…the hours she and her family would listen to radio serials or concerts. Her father, as his health declined, would count on the radio to keep him company as his family kept the farm going. At dinner he would catch them up on the goings-on around the world. In fact, it was during one of those dinner news sessions that he talked about post World War Germany and the up-and-coming politician by the name of Hitler. If everyone had been paying as much attention as her father…

With a sigh she turned off the radio. She knew it was dangerous to be caught listening to one. Their radio, like most of the radios in the area, had been confiscated early in the war. The Germans didn't want them to listen in on how the war was progressing and it was obvious that the BBC was sending coded messages in its programs. A few people gave up their bulky console radios to make it look like they were complying, while they hid their smaller wireless radios. It was those smaller radios that found their way to the Dupre's cisterns when they needed repair. It was a twist of fate that brought this particular trade to Nettie's attention.

In 1939, right before the war broke out, Nettie's Uncle Jean Paul had passed away. He had been the local electronics repairman and fixed radios and various other electronic equipment out of a small shop in the village. After his death the shop was cleaned out and sold. His widow, Aunt Elita, the younger sister to Nettie's mother, asked if she could store the remaining merchandise in one of the empty shacks on their farm until she could arrange to sell them. Unfortunately, the war broke out and the parts lay forgotten for months until they realized they were the only spare equipment available anywhere, for not only were the radios confiscated, so were any available parts.

Her vocation was selected for her when a friend of her aunt's appeared on her doorstep asking if Nettie could fix her radio. And to her own surprise, she was able to get it working again. After that she decided that she did indeed have some talent for electronics and would keep the fledgling, illegal business. The electronic parts for radios were separated out and placed in the hidden cupboard in the work shed. The rest of the electronic equipment was carefully wrapped up and packed into two empty wooden Calvados brandy barrels. The barrels, branded with the identifying words "Dupre's Finest" were then tucked away in the corner of the top shelf in the distillery. While she had found a way to hide the radio parts, she realized that she had to work out a safe system to receive deliveries and return the radios.

After several discarded ideas, she finally came up with one that seemed sensible, and that plan had worked for the last two years. It worked like this: A few people 'in the know' would place a radio they had obtained from someone they knew and trusted and placed it in the cistern under cover of darkness. They would then tie a ribbon on her bicycle when it was either parked behind the library or parked elsewhere when Lily was running errands. Nettie would go that night to pick it up and repair it as soon as possible. Sometimes she was unable to do anything to get it working again and it was happening more and more often as her spare parts were running out. When she completed all that she could, she would tie the same ribbon into her hair and wear it to work. The radio was invariably picked up that same night. She never asked for payment, but most of the time something would appear, like a pound of coffee or sugar on her desk or at the Dupre home.

She gently wrapped the radio back up and hid it back in the floor space. After locking the shed she knew that it was still early and there were plenty of household chores left for her to do. She knew the laundry was soaking in tubs on the porch so she decided to tackle that job and get it out of the way. She used the agitator for the more general dirty clothes. For those items with stains or especially dirty, Nettie scrubbed with a brush or used the wash board. While one load was washing, she rinsed and ran another load through the wringer. Before too long her back and arms ached and sweat ran down her face. It was late afternoon before she hung up the last of the washing on the lines set up in the back of the farmhouse. After dumping the wash water, she leaned the tubs against the front porch to dry before putting them away in the cellar. She sat on the porch steps, leaning back on her elbows and relaxing in the late afternoon sun. She sighed, enjoying the feel of her damp clothing in the warm weather. She let her relaxed mind think back to earlier days of doing the laundry with her sister, Terese. The story-telling and gossiping between the two sisters had made the chore go by quickly and in warm weather it was a wonderful way to cool down. Even though her sister had been her junior by eleven years, they had been unusually close, or at least she had thought so up to the day she had disappeared with their brother, Pierre. Now she tried not to think of her, or of Pierre. To focus her mind on other things, she scrambled to her feet and went into the kitchen to see if Nana had started supper yet. She had said things would be ready in a half an hour and asked if Nettie could locate her mother in the orchard. The assignment was a welcomed diversion and she set off down the path to the distillery. Nearing the building and seeing the door open, she called her mother's name and was answered by "I'm in here." She entered the cool, dark interior and breathed deeply of its smell. Even though it had not held Calvados brandy in years, it still reeked of the smell. Her mother was high up on a ladder pulling out bushel baskets that had been placed on an upper shelf. She handed them off to Nettie who gently stacked them on the floor.

"I guess I need to get these out and cleaned. The apples will be ready to pick in a few weeks, so warn your friends, Nett."

Her daughter laughed. "No need, they have already started to ask when the apples would be ready."

"Good, good, I think we will have quite a crowd this year. It would not serve any purpose if the fruit went to waste." Climbing down the ladder she continued, "You know Nett, maybe we could put up some brandy. Maybe clean out all the equipment, assemble the stills. We have all the barrels we would need…" Eulalie Dupre stared dreamily off into space, her work gloves resting on her hips. "Bring this place back to life. I remember when your father and my father built this distillery; it was right after we married and it was the most modern distillery in the whole area. Produced the best brandy in the area. We sold it all over and in a few fancy restaurants in Paris, too."

"Mother, we just can't, we just can't," said Nettie as she slumped, suddenly weary, against the thick, wooden wall.

Her mother hung her head. "I know, I know. We don't have the time," and then she sighed, "or the energy."

"Not to mention that the Germans would just steal it anyway," Nettie added bitterly.

"Now, now, they paid us a good price when we sold our remaining stock to them," chided her mother.

"Hmmm, what do you mean 'we'? I don't remember seeing any of that money."

"I'm sure they had their reasons, Nett."

"And I'd like to hear it."

"Nett, if it makes any difference to you, when your grandmother and I are gone, the farm will be yours. I just wish I could do a better job of taking care of it for you."

"What about Pierre and Terese?" Nettie asked.

"You are the one who has stayed and worked on the farm, plus you are the oldest child. I know it's been…hard. With…everything." She let her voice trail off. After a moment of silence she added, "Oh, and Nett, I'm afraid the seedlings are pretty much gone. Since we can't get any new wire fencing and the old fencing is falling apart, the rabbits have been helping themselves."

"Just make sure they show their ration cards," joked Nettie.

"That's my Nett" her mother said as she patted her daughter's cheek. "Here, help me with this box of canning jars I found and I'll go get washed up for supper."

Nettie helped steady the heavy box of glass jars and promised to bring the other box with her when she came in, but right now she wanted to stay behind and look for more baskets.

After a look around the building, Nettie ascertained there were no more baskets to be found and sat down on an old wooden chair that had been left inside the abandoned building. After years of being unused, the dust and dirt had gained a firm foothold in the interior of the distillery. She scuffed her work shoes on the floor and watched the dust rise up and settle in the filtered sunshine that flooded through the open door. She looked around her at the empty shelves and the barrels, also empty, stacked against the walls. Anger filled her at the pathetic state of the farm and she couldn't even direct that anger at the Germans. Oh yes, the Germans had paid a handsome price right after they marched into their village; goodness knows the drunk for a Commandant had consumed much of it himself. Her anger was aimed directly at the persons not there to share the work of keeping their livelihood alive. Her brother and sister had instead waited for Nettie, her mother, and Nana to attend the funeral of a close friend, and in their absence sold the entire stock to the German Army. The next night, the trio, still unaware that the stores had been emptied, had gone to bed early only to awaken to find Pierre and Teresa missing. A note had been placed at the table stating simply that they felt an obligation to fight for the freedom of France and they would be in touch. And would they please forgive them for selling the brandy and taking the car.

Mother and Nana had cried for days over concern for the two youngest children. Nettie, however, had burned with anger. She had wanted to leave Blanc Fleur, but had come home after graduation from university and stayed to help until her younger siblings would be able to take over the farm. And now they were gone, gone with two of their bigger assets, the brandy and the car. And here they were, nearly three years later. They worked from sun-up to sun-down, seven days a week. They had been forced to sell off the dairy herd, the orchard was just surviving, and the future was slipping away. Fight for France? Pierre had been a twenty two-year-old man, but to take his eighteen-year-old sister? Obviously, he hadn't been thinking straight. A few notes had been passed along to them stating that they were fine and hoped the war would be over soon. They hadn't heard from them in six months and when Nettie's anger ebbed, worry crept into her mind.

Realizing that supper would be ready, Nettie walked out of the distillery and shut the door behind her. As she passed through the clearing she strolled by one of the wells and lazily ran her hand over the rough stones. So this would all be hers someday. It wasn't what she had always wanted. She had grown up dreaming of going to exciting places and teaching in exotic lands. She had escaped briefly, living in Paris and attending teachers' college. While there she had tasted the culture and diversity of the city and it had only fueled her desire to leave her corner of the world.

While in Paris, there had been one young man in whom Nettie had more than a passing interest. Louis, a native of the city of Caen, had attended the same teachers' college and graduated at the same time as Nettie; however, he immediately set out on his own adventure and had obtained a teaching position in Quebec, Canada. Nettie had decided to return home as her father's already fragile health was failing and a position was available in the same village school she had attended in her youth. Louis would write often, and in 1934, soon after her father passed away, sailed home for a summer visit. He begged her to accompany him back to North America. He already feared the trouble brewing in nearby Germany and worried about the future of France. But what could she do? Her brother Pierre was just 16 and her sister only 12; they couldn't very well run the farm without her help. No, she told Louis, perhaps when Pierre was older and had mastered the art of producing Calvados that he was learning from neighbors now that father was gone. Just two years, she promised him, just two years.

Nettie would often replay their last meeting in her mind. On his way to Cherbourg to catch the ship heading back to North America, he had stopped by the Dupre farmhouse. Nettie had sat on the porch swing all night so as not to miss him. Hard as she had tried not to, she had fallen asleep and was awakened by the jingle of harnesses and clopping of hooves. Opening her eyes, all she could see were two points of light coming down the road. They were the lanterns attached to the wagon that was carrying Louis to the docks. She had sprung to her feet and straightened her bedraggled clothing as best she could before the wagon pulled up to the farmhouse. And so, they said their good-byes in the early morning hours of that August nine years earlier. The letters they promised each other continued but because of the on-coming war, travel was considered risky and he had never returned for so much as a visit.

Finally in 1939, Nettie decided that her brother at nearly twenty years of age was old enough to manage the farm and informed them that she would be leaving for Canada as soon as possible. Her money that she had saved purchased a one way ticket to New York City and from there she would make her way to Quebec by train or, by this time, she would walk if she had to. Her date to set sail was September 1st, 1939. Her trunk was packed and they were loading the car before dawn that morning when her friend and fellow teacher, Anna, rode up on her old plow horse. She was out of breath and near tears. Nettie teased her about being so late for the send off when Anna interrupted her with the news that war had broken out in Poland. The sailing had to be delayed while they anxiously watched the events unfold around them. Hoping for the best, Nettie had decided to wait a few months before attempting to leave. How could she leave her family behind during these times? The situation worsened quickly as France fell early in 1940 and by the fall Germans had set up shop in their town and along the cliffs. Nettie still had hopes to leave during the occupation; after all, what was one young woman worth to the German army. She had written to Louis and told him of her circumstances. She never heard back. It was not long before certain groups of people began to disappear. The Jews, those with communist views, were the first to fade into the background. Of course Blanc Fleur was hardly affected at first as it only counted a handful of Jews amongst its inhabitants and politics had little place in this farming community. It would take the enforced "work assignments" of early 1943 to wake the populace up to the insidious evil that had come into its midst.

Those selected to work for the Third Reich were mostly young and male, but some young women where forced to leave as well. It was during the first round of "selection" that the young men of Blanc Fleur started to disappear. Of course, Pierre and Terese had already left the area long before the call-up for work assignments had started. Perhaps he had a good reason to leave, her grandmother would tell her, but all Nettie could think about was how close she herself had come to leaving. It should have been her that left, she was the one who had worked so hard and sacrificed her life for her siblings and here they had run off as soon as they could. Not only had they left her in charge on a farm she didn't want, they had taken the family car, sold the entire stock of brandy, and helped themselves to the money she had saved for her future in Canada.

Her face reflected her angry thoughts as she stormed toward the house. Before she opened the door she forced herself to take a deep breath and force a smile to her lips.

Chapter 5

On that Monday morning Nettie carefully tied the red ribbon on the end of her braid. She had placed the repaired radio in the cistern the night before and figured that whomever had placed it there would pick it up that night. She was curious to know who owned such a beautiful and unusual item, but she couldn't very well ask around.

The day was cloudy and threatened rain. She said good-bye to her mother and Nana and headed to the garage to fetch her bicycle and headed off to school. The older women were canning the last of the summer beans that day, a job from which Nettie was relieved to be excused.

She hoped the always unpredictable weather would improve in time for the apple harvest. Today she would tell those interested that the picking would take place in three weeks. For the last two years friends and relatives of the Dupres had pitched in with the harvesting. The chore of harvesting apples from the acres of apple trees along with the day-to-day responsibilities was too much for the three women.

As she pedaled along the road she began to think about how she could avoid the new Commandant during the hours she spent at work in the village. The thought of quitting or finding a position in another town crossed her mind but she had to quickly dismiss those alternatives. Her family needed the income too much for her to quit and commuting to another town would be impossible because of the lack of an automobile and the trains that rarely ran on time. Thoughts of the new Commandant unfortunately brought up memories of the previous one. It was on a dreary day, much like this one in the fall of 1941, that Nettie had ridden into the village and, pressed for time, rode past the school without looking for her colleagues whom usually gathered on the stoop before class. If she had just glanced in the direction she would have witnessed soldiers, weapons drawn, entering the main entrance to the school. Nettie, hearing the 9 a.m. chime of the church bells, quickened her pace and, finding the library gate open, rode into the garden. She placed the bicycle against the wall and hurried to the street without taking the time to talk to Lily.

She had just reached the front gate of the courtyard when she heard shouts of people and the screams of the school children. Confused, she continued into the courtyard, her eyes on the school. Nothing appeared wrong on the outside of the building and she put her hand out to take hold of the handrail of the front stairs. Before she could do this, she heard a single voice shrieking "Help me! Help me!" and a thump as the owner of that voice fell against the main door and it flew open. It was Sister Pauline, a young nun that had been recently assigned to Blanc Fleur. Nettie's surprise turned to horror as the young woman ran down the steps and a dozen soldiers were close behind her in pursuit. One of the soldiers pushed Nettie aside with such force that she fell backwards, landing hard on the cobblestones. She looked up just as one of the men lifted his weapon to his shoulder and with a single pull on the trigger struck Sister Pauline in the back. The young woman lunged forward, flung against the wrought iron gate. Slowly she sank to the ground. As the soldiers stared at what they had done, Marie-Claire rushed by them and knelt by her friend. She took her in her arms and whispered comforting words into her ear. One of the men went to stand over them, took out his pistol and shot Sister Pauline in the forehead. The air filled with Marie-Claire's heart-rending wails. The soldier, still standing over them, pointed his pistol at Marie-Claire and looked over his shoulder at a higher-ranking officer. The officer shook his head from side to side and the soldier shrugged and lowered his gun and walked away with the rest.

Nettie struggled to her feet and glanced up at the school. Her eyes were directed to the windows that were filled with the children and teachers that had witnessed the whole incident as it had unfolded beneath them.

For the rest of her life Nettie knew she would always remember the sight of Marie-Claire sitting on the cold, wet cobbles and covered in her friend's blood; the silence of the surreal scene only broken by the sound of her grief.

Several weeks later it was learned that Sister Pauline's father was involved in the Paris Underground and had been caught directing food supplies to the freedom fighters. It was by direct order of the Fuhrer himself that the entire family had been executed.

A week after the murder of one of their own, Mr. LaPierre, the principal of the school, had quietly asked each of the teachers and support staff to come to the basement meeting room at 10 am. To avoid having the Germans and even the students ask questions about what they were doing, they were to slip away without explanation.

One by one they made their way to the basement. When all 18 persons had arrived, Mr. LaPierre stood up to address them. He looked down at their expectant faces, some young, some old, all showing the strain of the last week. He cleared his throat and, speaking softly, began. "I have asked you to meet me here today to talk to you about the great evil that has descended upon our village, actually our whole country. I am sure you know that we teachers are not going to save the country. I think all we can do is hope to survive these dark days, may they be few in number, ahead." He sighed and paced around the group searching for his next words. "I have a feeling some of you or someone close to you, has been or will be in the future, involved in what the Germans consider to be illegal activity." He stopped and looked at the group and continued, "The only way we will survive is if we all band together and help each other out. Actually, I want to take it one step further, I want us to take a pledge."

"What kind of pledge?" questioned Margarethe.

"I want us to pledge three things to each other. One, that you will never divulge to anyone, even to others in this group, any gossip, hearsay, or any activity that you yourself see to another living soul. Two, you will do anything in your power to ensure your own or another's in this group, survival. That may mean that we compromise our own personal or moral beliefs." He looked at Sister Marie-Claire who slowly nodded in agreement. "And third, and this may be the hardest of all, you will place your complete trust in one another. I know most of you have this trust with your families and close friends, but now you must put aside all your petty disagreements and keep the greater good foremost in your mind. You may see another do something you don't agree with or even looks suspicious, but you must believe they are doing it with your best interest in mind. Along with that is that in every thing you do, you must keep the others in mind." When he had stopped talking he looked at the group. For a few moments no one spoke, each lost in his or her own thoughts.

Sister Marie-Claire finally spoke up. "I agree, we must all stick together. Depend on one another. I know that one in my 'profession' needs to count on God, and I do," she hastily added, "but I also know what they did to Sister Pauline. I agree that if we can vow to look out for each other, it would be with the approval of our Lord."

The others nodded in agreement. "OK," enthused Mr. LaPierre. "Then let us put our right hands in and pledge like they do in that book 'The Three Musketeers' and swear 'All for one, and one for all.'"

They each stuck their right hands into the center of the table, one on top of another. Mr. LaPierre put his left hand under the pile and his right on top. "Are we agreed to the terms I told you before?" All heads nodded. "OK. Will it be 'all for one, and one for all'?"

"Amen," was the one simple word reply from one and all.

After a moment of silence, Clea spoke up and said quietly. "As Benjamin Franklin, the Eighteenth Century American Ambassador to France said, 'We must all hang together, or assuredly we shall all hang separately.'"

Nettie wondered if she was the only one with chills running down her back.

And so, they had each and all kept their word for the last three years. They were all still alive. And they had indeed helped each other out. When it became known that Francois' predilection could get him deported or shot, Margarethe had arranged for him to marry her widowed aunt Cat. Called 'Cat' because she always seemed to have a dozen of those creatures in her home. To the surprise of many the marriage of convenience had been a happy one. While Margarethe didn't approve of Francois or his lifestyle, she was happy to see they enjoyed each other's company. Most of the gestures were less dramatic, merely trading food items or encouraging each other through the bad times. Most important to Nettie, they had never asked what had happened at her farm that day in June. Her mind cleared to the present as she passed through the wrought iron gates that lead to the school courtyard. The blood of Sister Pauline had long since been washed away, but she found herself still glancing from the cobblestones back up to the windows of the school.

Chapter 6

The first full week of the new Commandant's tenure had passed smoothly, reflected Nettie as she rode that Friday morning into town. Frederick, as the Commandant's aide, had shown his new master around the village and introduced him to its inhabitants. On Tuesday he had made a visit to the school. To the surprise of the teachers, the Commandant had arrived on the premises wearing gray uniform trousers and a crisp white dress shirt with black, non-regulation dress shoes. And came without a sidearm.

With Frederick leading the way, he started his tour on the first floor and finished in Nettie's classroom. He observed Marie-Claire demonstrating math problems on the blackboard while Nettie busied herself at her desk. When the lesson was over, the Commandant strode to the front of the class and commended the young scholars on their math skills. Then to their surprise he added "Do you have any questions for me?"

Nettie and Marie-Claire held their breath, realizing what a dangerous question this could be to a group of fourth graders. The children sat uncomfortably in their chairs; they knew that while this man was dressed as their fathers sometimes were, he was the leader of the enemies that had taken over their village. An uncomfortable silence settled over the room. Just when Nettie started to wonder if she should speak up to relieve the tension, Algeron, a boy that Nettie had to remind to be silent during tests, spoke up.

"Do you have a horse?"

The Commandant, apparently also relieved to have a question posed to him, responded, "No, but I did have one growing up. I used to ride him in the fields outside of the town I grew up in. I called him Donner. I believe his name in French would be Tonnerre. He was a dark bay with a large white star on his forehead."

Pursuing this line of questioning, Algeron ventured forth with, "Was he a big horse?"

"Yes…no…overfed I guess you could say." And with that he let forth with a sharp, high-pitched laugh that startled everyone in the room. After a moment of uneasy silence, another student, Henri asked, "Do you have a dog?"

"Yes, I have a spaniel named Fidel."

"Do you have a ca…"

"OK, students," interrupted Nettie. She knew the children would go on until they had named every animal roaming the earth. "I'm sure the Commandant is a busy man and has other places to visit."

Taking the hint gracefully, the Commandant thanked the students and the teachers for their time and wished them well before leaving the room. It was with great relief that Nettie closed the door after him and gave Marie-Claire a weak smile before turning to the students and thanking them for behaving so well during his visit. A silent thanks went to Algeron for speaking up and asking a question. She would let him talk all he wanted during the next test, she was that grateful.

As she had the Friday before, she turned off onto the dirt lane that led to the cemetery. She did not normally visit the graves so often; however, for some reason in the last few years, she had found it to be a place that she could go and reflect. Previously she would have traveled to the cliffs for peace and quiet, but now her cliffs were off limits to civilians.

She picked a handful of the late summer wildflowers and placed a small bouquet at each headstone. She sat down on the soft earth and pulled her knees up to her chin. She rested her cheek on her knees and shut her eyes. Breathing deeply, she took in the sweet smell of mowed grass and the sounds of twittering birds. So peaceful. What if she had gone to Canada? Who would visit so often, her mother? Nana? No, they rarely came into the village, spending their time working on the farm. Nettie figured that it, too, was her responsibility. She looked at the stone belonging to her brother, Guillaume. She well remembered that day. It was wet and cold, as it often was in Normandy. It was a November day in 1918 and they had sat in the front pew of the Normanesque town church. After Father Girard intoned the funeral mass, they had followed the small coffin, carried by four male members of her family, down the steps and through the streets to the city gate.

At the gate most members of the sad parade dispersed while the close family continued on past the gate and to the narrow lane. The bare limbs of the trees lining the lane stretched eerily overhead and Nettie clasped the hand of Nana more tightly. Her mother clung to her brother-in-law, Jean-Paul. Not only did she have the death of her eldest child to bear, but the telegram that had arrived just the day before bore the news that her husband, missing for two weeks, had been located in a convalescent hospital. He had been badly gassed in one of the trenches on the western front of the war. No identification was found of him and he had not been able to tell the hospital staff who he was. They were unable to say for sure if he would recover.

It was with this impossible burden on her small shoulders that Eulalie Dupre led the mourners to bury her firstborn. Nettie stood between her mother and Nana beside the grave. Was it just two days ago that she was playing with Guillaume in the orchard? They had been called in to supper and while Nettie had dug into her meal with usual relish, Guillaume had started to complain of not feeling well. Nana, thinking he was just tired, sent him up to bed for a nap. Surprisingly he did not complain as he mounted the stairs to his room. Her mother was sleeping in the downstairs bedroom as baby brother Pierre was teething and his cranky cries kept the whole house awake. Nettie helped Nana with the evening chores and went to bed early.

Sometime in the middle of the night she awoke to find Benoit, the handyman, standing over her with a lamp. He set the lamp down and, picking her up, carried her down the narrow hallway to the stairs. The door to her brother's room was open and several people were standing around Guillaume's small bed. Nettie struggled to open her eyes. "What's wrong?" she questioned drowsily.

Benoit didn't answer her and continued on his way down the stairs and then to Nana's bedroom. He placed her on the big bed and pulled the blankets up to her chin. Only then did he speak. "Stay here child. Until morning." Nettie could hear baby Pierre's deep breathing coming from the crib next to the bed. She closed her sleepy eyes and did not wake up until the streams of the weak November sun came through the bedroom window. She stirred, confused as to why she was in Nana's bed. Sounds of sobbing seemed to be coming from upstairs. Curious, she glanced at the crib to find the baby sleeping peacefully for the first time in days. Feeling the need to be quiet, she opened the bedroom door and peeked around the kitchen. No one was there. She heard people moving around the living room so she crept to the door leading from the kitchen to the living room and opened it slowly. She found her mother sobbing in Aunt Elita's arms and another man that she recognized as Doctor Farve hanging his head and saying how sorry he was that nothing could be done. It was then her aunt noticed Nettie standing there and held out her arms to her. This gesture somehow frightened Nettie. Something was horribly wrong and instinct told her the answer of what had happened was up those stairs. In a quick dash she skirted Aunt Elita's arms and ran up the stairs before the adults could catch her.

The door to her brother's room was open and Nana and Uncle Jean-Paul sat on chairs next to the bed.

There was a form in the bed, but it was covered with one of her mother's white sheets. Nettie ran up to the side of the bed and reached for the sheet to pull it off the inert form. Her uncle grabbed her arm and lifted her up to take her down the stairs when Nana stopped him with, "Put her down. If she were going to catch the influenza, she would have by now. She needs to say goodbye." Her uncle dutifully put her down and Nettie stood at the side of the bed while Nana picked up the corners of the sheet and revealed her brother's face. She looked down at the peaceful face, crowned by his tousled blonde hair. "Is he dead?" she whispered.

"Yes, my love, he is," answered Nana.

"Why?"

"He caught the influenza. You remember me telling you we couldn't go into town because of people being sick? Well, this is what they had."

"Did they all die too?"

"No, but a lot of them did." With that she covered his face back up and gently led her down the stairs.

For the rest of the day the farm was full of activity. Several people came to lend their support, most staying outside as they wished to avoid contracting the deadly disease. A woman came to help Nana with the body and a casket was brought in which to place him. It was to be kept sealed in the living room for fear of spreading the disease if they took it into town for the night. The funeral would take place the next day. It was that same evening a knock came at the door. It was the delivery boy from the local telegraph office. He knew of the death in the family and left the message under a stone on the front porch before beating a hasty retreat.

Eulalie retrieved the letter and handed it to Nana. With shaking hands, Nana opened the envelope and after reading its contents, sank into the nearest chair. "What is it Mother? It's Gilly, isn't it?"

Her mother nodded. "It says he is in a hospital. He was gassed in the trenches and they don't know if he will recover."

It was the last thing her mother needed to hear that awful day. Nettie put her childish arms around her mother, but she didn't say anything, as she knew no words could be of comfort.

Silently she made her way to the gravesite and listened to the last prayers before the grave was filled in. On the way out, her Uncle Jean-Paul took her aside and holding her at arms length said, "Nettie, you are the oldest now. It is up to you to take care of your mother and help her and your grandmother until your father comes home." Numbly, eight-year-old Nettie had nodded her reply.

Nettie sighed and absently picked at the grass covering her father's grave. More to herself than to the deceased spirit of her father she whispered, "I looked after Mother and Nana as best as an eight-year-old could until you came home. And then I looked after you. And I looked after Pierre and Terese. And then I had to look after Uncle Jean-Paul's business. Just when I thought I could leave for a life of my own, Pierre and Terese ran away. And things here…" She stopped as a tear ran down her cheek.

"Mademoiselle Dupre, how lovely to see you again."

Nettie whipped her head around so quickly she was momentarily dizzy. When the world stopped spinning she could see the Commandant advancing in her direction with Frederick striding beside him.

Panic was the first sensation Nettie felt. Realizing it was much too late to hide or run away, she decided a quick retreat was the best she could hope for. It was not to be. Before she could struggle to her feet, he gently shoved her shoulder downward. Catching her off balance, she fell backwards and landed hard on her backside.

Seeing what he had done, he apologized. "I am so sorry, Mademoiselle Dupre, are you OK?"

Nettie assured him she was just fine and took the opportunity to scooch back a few more inches from the men standing over her.

The Commandant took a seat on the ground a few feet away from her while Frederick tipped his cap and uttered a non-committal "Mademoiselle" and went to stand near the cemetery gate.

For what seemed like an eternity the Commandant merely looked at Nettie, his face expressionless but his dark gray eyes seemed to be drilling into her soul. Feeling uncomfortable, she dropped her eyes and picked at the grass once again.

"Would these be relatives of yours?"

Lifting her eyes, Nettie answered while pointing at each headstone. "My grandfather, my father, and my older brother."

"Hmmm. 1918. Did your brother die in the influenza epidemic?"

"Yes. One moment he was fine and the next morning he was dead."

The Commandant nodded his head slowly. "I heard of such stories. It struck the young and healthy hardest. Luckily it wasn't bad in my town. Did his death make you an only child?"

"No, it made me the oldest. I have a younger brother and sister," she answered simply.

"I hope I can meet them soon, or have I already met them?"

Looking him straight in the eyes Nettie stated, "I don't know where they are."

"Oh." He shifted uncomfortably and continued on with what he hoped was a safer topic. "And your father?"

"The Great War."

"But the stone says 1934," the Commandant pointed out.

"He was gassed in the trenches. It just took sixteen years for him to die."

This time the Commandant dropped his eyes before getting to his feet and holding out his hand. "Come, Mademoiselle Dupre, it is time for us to leave."

Fearing snubbing the Commandant, she grasped his hand while he pulled her to her feet. Nettie and the Commandant walked toward the village engaged in polite conversation while Frederick rode behind on Nettie's bicycle. Just inside the gate Frederick dismounted and the three continued on, walking three abreast. At the sight of the Commandant, his aide, and Nettie Dupre walking together, people stopped to gape and whisper among themselves.

They were passing a pair of sisters, students at the school, oblivious to who was walking behind them, chatting excitedly to each other when the Commandant stopped and started conversing with them. Nettie strained to hear what they were saying but she quickly realized they were speaking in a German dialect with which she was not familiar. But from what she could understand it seemed like an innocuous conversation about where the girls were from. After a few moments the Commandant excused himself and bid a goodbye to the girls.

Rejoining Nettie and Frederick he remarked, "Those girls are from a tiny village near where my Grandfather lived. I thought I recognized the dialect."

Nettie replied, "Trudi and Elsa were taken in by the Collier family several years ago. I believe their mother was Madam Collier's sister."

The Commandant merely nodded and offhandedly added, "I wonder if they know their village no longer exists?"

"Was it bombed?" Nettie asked innocently.

"No, but its inhabitants were predominantly Jewish," he commented as he continued on his way down the street.

Nettie's mouth formed a perfect O at the implications of what had just transpired before her.

She glanced at Frederick walking on the other side of her. His head was down, seemingly oblivious to the whole conversation. Thankfully they had reached the gate to the schoolyard and Nettie and the Commandant turned into the courtyard while Frederick promised to take the bicycle to the library for Nettie.

Nettie waited on the steps of the school until the bell rang and watched as the students piled in the doors. Odd, while she had just seen Trudi and Elsa in the street, obviously on their way to school, they were nowhere to be seen.

To Clea standing next to her, Nettie mentioned seeing the Klein sisters on the way to school and what the Commandant had said. Clea looked concerned but shrugged her shoulders and entered the building without saying a word.

Later, after school, Nettie strolled up the street to the library to fetch her transportation home. To her surprise Lily was waiting outside the library door and motioned Nettie to come closer.

"What's wrong, Lily?"

"Maybe nothing. I just saw the Commandant walk by. Would you walk up the street and see where he went?"

Nettie looked at Lily like she had lost her mind but said, "Well, sure," and walked but a half a block and found the Commandant knocking on the Collier door. Seeing Nettie, he stopped knocking and came back out to the street to talk to her.

He thrust out a small package he was carrying. "I wanted to give them this." It consisted of several bars of chocolate tied together by a red ribbon. "But no one seems to be home. Would you know where they may be?" he asked, looking intently into her face.

She stared back and answered honestly, "No, Herr Commandant, I wouldn't know where they are."

He searched her face for a moment before reaching for her hand and placing the chocolate bars in it with the words, "If you see them, please give them these." Nettie merely nodded and turned and walked back to the library as quickly as possible. Nettie found Lily waiting for her just outside the door. Nettie motioned her inside and after inquiring if they were alone, told Lily what had happened.

Lily thanked her but said nothing about why she was so interested in the Commandant's presence in the area.

Before she left, Nettie handed her the chocolate and asked her to give it to the Colliers if she should see them. With that Nettie fetched her bicycle and with considerable relief left town.

Chapter 7

The next day, Saturday, was market day. Market day had always been a day of socializing for the citizens of Blanc Fleur. It was not unusual for the people in the outlying farms to come into town only during market days and at no other time. If it were not for Nettie's job, she herself would only come to town on rare occasions. Like most farmers, their garden, chickens, and orchard supplied most of what they needed. Usually all three of the Dupres would make the trek into town and socialize with the other farmers, and her mother and Nana would visit with other villagers that Nettie saw almost every day.

It was a beautiful August morning and Nettie was looking forward to seeing some of the farmers she knew would be there that day. Plus, she was curious to find out about the Klein sisters. What did she know about them? Not much, she realized, when she thought about it. When they arrived in 1938 people had been told they came from a small town in Germany and their parents had been ill. The mother was supposedly the sister of Madam Collier, but Nettie didn't see much resemblance between the red headed, blue eyed Madam Collier and the two blond, brown-eyed girls. Trudi, the eldest, was sixteen now and in her last year of schooling. Else was twelve and small for her age. Nettie had had Else in her fourth grade class, but she didn't really know either girl very well. No one seemed to. Madam Collier had always claimed they were fragile in health and couldn't play often with other children, least they fell ill. When they first arrived, a few people expressed surprise that Madam Collier had a sister, but since she was originally from Paris they had to admit they didn't know much about her family. Monsieur Collier, a native to Blanc Fluer, never would talk about his new charges. But his silence was laughed off to the fact that with his own three young daughters, it made for six women against one man and he had given up talking until the girls left home.

She was finished with her breakfast and getting her shoes on when her mother mentioned that she and Nana would stay home and catch up on some chores and, slipping her daughter some money, would she buy some flowers for Nana's birthday the next day?

Nettie was disappointed in not having company going into town, but she picked up the market basket and Nana's list of what they needed and set off on foot.

The two miles passed swiftly and soon Nettie was entering the village gates. The first people she met up with were her Aunt Elita and her teenage daughter, Aimee. Together they walked toward the center of the town where the market stalls were set up.

"How is business, Nett?" asked her aunt.

Nettie, knowing exactly what she was referring to, asked in a low whisper about the unusual radio she had worked on the weekend before.

"Hmmm, silver and mahogany you say? No, I can honestly say I have never seen anything like that, and I have been in most folks' homes at one time or another. It must have come from somewhere else. But it was broken you say? Doesn't sound like something someone would be careless with."

"No, it wasn't broken, just needed a little tightening here and there," answered her niece.

"It just seems odd," her aunt mused. Changing the subject she asked, "Are the apples ready to be picked yet? Aimee and I are ready to come over, just let us know."

"Another two or three weeks. That's what Mother and Nana are doing, getting ready for the big day."

Together the three of them started to inspect the produce of the first vegetable stand they came to. Their conversation was interrupted by a crash behind them. They turned to find that Frederick had tripped over several crates of squash. Fortunately, the only thing broken seemed to be a few crates. Several people laughed at the sight of the tall German boy sprawled on the ground. It wasn't the first time that Frederick had landed face first in the market place. Several vendors had talked about approaching Commandant Neumann and requesting that his aide be banned from the market place. But because they feared the Commandant, and underneath it all liked the boy, nothing was done.

After the initial outburst of laughter, an uneasy silence fell over the crowd. Doubtlessly they were recalling the previous Commandant who would curse and beat Frederick with his riding crop and anyone else who tried to help the boy. However, this Commandant helped Frederick to his feet and inquired of any injuries he may have obtained. He then pitched in to help Frederick pick up the squash that had rolled free of their crates. Citizens that helped where rewarded with a smile and a nod instead of a curse and a beating. Nettie, upon feeling a freed squash that had rolled onto the toe of her shoe, swiftly bumped it under the stall she was standing before. She remained planted to her spot and after a moment of watching what was going on, she turned and resumed her shopping. She tried to ignore the murmurs around her.

"Can you believe it?" asked one.

"He seems different from the last one," stated another.

"I guess we won't send him to the Dupre orchard," teased another. Hearing that comment, Nettie turned around and caught the eye of a man she knew only by name. Seeing her angry face, he shut up and he and his friend walked away. Nettie went back to looking over the blossoms displayed by the flower peddler.

"They are beautiful flowers, are they not?" She stiffened at the familiar German voice.

She turned toward him slowly and looked up into those gray eyes that always seemed to be fixed into her brown ones.

"Yes, they are very lovely this time of year," she answered simply. And then feeling like she owed those inquisitive eyes an explanation she added "I need some for my grandmother's birthday tomorrow."

"I would think farmers would have flowers galore on their farms."

"We don't have time for…" she struggled for the proper words… "such frivolous plants."

"I see. I wish your grandmother the happiest of birthdays. I don't believe I have had the pleasure of meeting her yet."

"No, my mother and grandmother must work very hard on our farm," Nettie replied as she reached for a colorful bouquet and passed a few francs to the vendor and turned to leave. However, the Commandant was not so easily dislodged from her side and followed her on to the next stall.

"Perhaps my aide could carry your basket?" he asked courteously.

She glanced at Frederick and shook her head. "I would prefer if my basket stayed upright, if you don't mind."

Frederick gave a wry grin from his position behind the Commandant. As she continued her shopping, the Commandant started to ask detailed questions about the fruits and vegetables that were on display. Nettie was hardly an expert in the area and in an attempt to get rid of the persistent man, made up answers when she didn't know the correct one. Judging from her aunt's occasional raised eyebrow, some answers were rather creative. However, the German never moved from her elbow.

After what seemed like an eternity, the Commandant was distracted by a few of his soldiers arguing with one of the vendors. Taking advantage of the situation, Nettie grabbed her aunt by the arm and shoved her cousin into a bakery shop. They made their way to the back door and stepped out into an alley and bid each other a hasty goodbye.

Nettie rounded the corner out of the alley and stepped out onto a small side street. She meant to take the side street all the way to the old wall and follow the wall to the road home, thereby reducing the chance of running into the Commandant again.

On the corner of the side street and the main street sat a small café and seated at a table were Francois, Clea, Anna, and Margarethe.

Seeing her, they shouted her name in unison. Nettie shushed them with a finger held to her lips. She advanced to their table and sat on an empty chair between Clea and Anna.

"What's the matter? That nasty Nazi following you around again?" joked Francois.

"Francois, be careful!" cautioned Margarethe who motioned to a pair of Germans enjoying a beer at a nearby table.

Nettie leaned into the table and in a hushed voice said, "He has been following me around the market for the last half hour. I finally ditched him by slipping into a bake shop."

"Anna here was telling us about Frederick's mishap. It was refreshing to hear that he did not beat his aide when he had his usual attack of the 'clumsy.'" Francois replied sarcastically.

"Maybe he won't be so bad," offered Anna. "Remember when he showed up at school and wasn't wearing his uniform? I think it was because he didn't want to frighten the children."

"Well, at least he is better looking," added Clea.

"Oh Clea!" Margarethe said with forced exasperation. The others laughed at Clea being, well, Clea. Margarethe continued, "I don't care what his motive was, and being a kraut, I'm sure he had one. I plan on staying as far away from him as I can, so I guess he is all yours Clea!"

Clea merely smiled mischievously.

"I can't figure out why they sent us a first lieutenant instead of a captain. What's the matter, doesn't Blanc Fleur rate high enough for a real Nazi?" complained Francois.

"Technically he is just a German solider, not a Nazi. I think the term Nazi is reserved for those special troops of Hitler," Margarethe offered.

Anna added, "That should make you feel even worse, not only do we not rate high enough for a captain, we don't even get a Nazi."

Francois thought for a minute before saying, "He may be a low ranking kraut, but that boy does come from money. I mean, he smokes real tobacco and I hear that car he drives around is his. And not only does he have nice clothes, he wears them wonderfully. Even I noticed *that*."

"I bet you did," laughed Clea.

Francois just smiled and mused, "Yep, that boy has money and undoubtedly, connections. How else would he get a cushy post like this? I wonder who he knows?"

Feeling safe with her friends, Nettie briefly told them about the incident between the Commandant and the Klein sisters the day before. She finished with, "Has anyone seen them?"

Anna and Margarethe shook their heads while Clea and Francois glanced at each other.

Francois answered with, "Rumor has it that they have…ah…left."

"All of them?" Asked Nettie.

"Yes, all."

"Did they leave on their own or were they helped by the Commandant?"

Francois gave her a long look before replying, "They left on their own."

Nettie sighed in relief.

To break the tension Francois spoke up. "Guess what Nett? Guess what I came across in my cupboard yesterday?"

"I am afraid to ask."

"I found a bottle of Dupre's finest Calvados Brandy!"

Surprised, Nettie answered, "Really? Even I don't have any."

"I have an idea. On the first Sunday after the town is liberated, we will all meet here and break it open. What do you say?" offered Francois.

"Sounds great," agreed Nettie. And the others expressed their approval. "I can't wait for that day," she said dreamily "Go into a restaurant and order anything I want, walk down the street without hearing that guttural Germanic language. And, best of all, being able to turn around without seeing that Commandant."

"Nett. Don't turn around, because guess who is coming towards us?" whispered Francois.

"You're kidding." answered an incredulous Nettie. But sure enough, in a second she could hear the sound of boots on cobblestones behind her.

"Ah, Mademoiselle Dupre, we can't seem to miss each other today."

Nettie glanced up into the now familiar gray eyes and announced, "I was just on my way Home," and jumped to her feet. As fast as she was, the Commandant beat her in the reach for her market basket.

"Then I shall carry this for you as far as the town gate."

Nettie realized the offer was not open to debate and decided to nod her approval to the arrangement. To her friends she bid goodbye and said she would see them Monday. If she had looked back she would have seen that their faces reflected their reactions, which ranged from amusement to honest concern.

Nettie walked as swiftly as she could with the Commandant striding beside her trying to engage her in polite conversation.

She was successful in blocking out his chatter until they reached the town gate and she turned to take her basket. She heard him say "Rolfe" and she looked up at him in confusion and repeated "Rolfe?"

"Yes. I said you may call me Rolfe." When she didn't answer he continued on. "It's my name. Rolfe."

Suddenly realizing how stupid he must think she was, she blushed in embarrassment. He grinned at the sight of her obvious discomfort, which suddenly made her angry. She grabbed the basket roughly out of his hands, causing her grandmother's flowers to spill out. They both reached down at the same time, knocking their heads together. He handed her the flowers while rubbing his left temple and exclaimed, "You sure are a hard-headed mademoiselle!"

"May I have my flowers please?" she asked, trying to hide her fury.

"Of course," he answered, his eyes dancing in merriment, gently placing the bouquet on top of the basket and then reached out to touch her shoulder.

"Don't touch me," she snapped and turned around and stomped off. He retracted his hand and watched her break into a run that she kept up until she was nearly home.

Chapter 8

The next two weeks passed by quickly. A beautiful Tuesday morning found a large group of teachers enjoying lunch on the front steps of the school. Their reasons for eating outside were actually twofold. One was to enjoy the pleasant weather while it lasted and the other was to keep an eye on the playing children. They were only allowed to play in the courtyard and there was always the danger of them becoming a nuisance to the soldiers.

"Have you asked Rolfe's permission for us to get together on Saturday yet?" inquired Anna.

Nettie snorted. "Have *I* asked *Rolfe*? I didn't realize everyone was on a first name basis with our captor, our overseer, our…our," she stormed.

Anna poked her in the ribs with her elbow. "I understand *you* are on a first name basis with the Commandant, or should I say *Rolfe*?"

Nettie jumped to her feet, red faced and hands clenched. "I do not call *that man* Rolfe or anything other than Herr Commandant. I try not to believe that he is human, much less someone took the time to name him!"

"We get the idea Nett," smoothed Margarethe. "Anna was just teasing. He has asked most of us to feel free to refer to him as Rolfe."

"Even *you*? After what you said the other week?" protested Nettie.

"Well, I never said I had taken him up on the offer to call him by his given name. I haven't and I won't. But look around you Nett, things are calmer, more relaxed since he arrived. You probably didn't notice since you live so far out of town, but things have improved."

Nettie gave Margarethe a long look and shook her head. True, they didn't have soldiers underfoot 24 hours a day at the farm, but she had noticed a difference the few hours she was in the village. The Commandant was often out walking around the village, visiting with shopkeepers and chatting with civilians. She wasn't sure if he was getting acquainted with his new territory or running for office. He also seemed to show up wherever she did—the market, schoolyard, church. However, after the market day incident, he would merely smile and nod, only talking if Nettie spoke first. Things may be better than before, but she harbored doubts that things were as benign as they appeared.

Breaking the silence, Marie-Claire said, "Maybe God has sent our village a righteous man."

"I hope not, as that would make God an employee of the Third Reich," chimed in Francois.

"Well, if he is, I know where I wish he would assign all of them," added Nettie.

"That is not for us to decide," Marie-Claire quietly replied.

To that Nettie and Francois rolled their eyes at each other. Nettie went on. "Actually, I wish he would come by so I could ask him about Saturday."

"That's a switch, usually he is looking for *you*. I wish he would look for *me*," Clea sighed.

"I wish he would too," Replied Nettie. A silence fell over the group. It hadn't escaped his or her attention that while he was friendly to everyone, Nettie was the main focus of his attention. And this worried them.

"Oh my God," gasped Anna, who was rewarded with a poke in the ribs for use of the 'G' word with students around. They all turned in the direction she was looking and they were all horrified by what they saw. For across the courtyard marched the Commandant with a small struggling child under his arm.

"Oh my," breathed Clea. "It's one of my kindergartners." She jumped up and hurried towards the Commandant and took custody of her wayward student. They could make out her apologizing profusely for the trouble her student had caused. Clea then grasped the child's collar and marched him past the group of teachers and into the school. The Commandant had turned and was walking back to Headquarters when Nettie figured it was as good a time to talk to him as any. She walked quickly across the courtyard and caught up with him on the landing of the main staircase.

"May I have a word with you, Herr Commandant?"

"Of course, but Fraulein Farve has already apologized for her student."

"It's not about that."

"Right this way, Fraulein Dupre." He made a gesture to place his hand on her shoulder, but Nettie, seeing it coming out of the corner of her eye, did a fast side step to avoid it. She then made sure she was just far enough ahead of him as she walked to his office as to be out of touch range. If he noticed, he did not show it. He opened his door and ushered her in. To her relief he only shut the door half way. At his bidding she sat down in one of the chairs in front of his desk, where she had sat on her initial visit with the Commandant. To her surprise and dismay, he sat in the chair next to her rather than behind the big desk. With his elbows on his knees, he leaned forward and asked her what he could do to help her.

"I need a permission for a large group of people to gather at my orchard this Saturday. It is time to harvest the apples and a group of us get together to do most of it in one day."

"You need a permit for that?" he asked, seeming surprised.

"Well, yes. I had to ask permission in past years, as Commandant Neumann was concerned about an insurrection or something going on whenever large groups of civilians got together. We would like to pick apples without worrying about soldiers showing up with guns and dogs," she finished bluntly with a touch of sarcasm.

"I see you have already eaten a few sour apples," he commented dryly.

She flushed. She hadn't meant to answer him like that. She had to be more careful of this man.

He went on without pause. "Of course you may have permission. I am new here so I am not sure what I am supposed to do. Here, let me put this in writing." He leaned forward and began to shuffle through the papers on his desk. "This Saturday you said?"

"Yes this Saturday."

It was then that a mound of folders and papers drew Nettie's eyes to an object that lay half buried. It was a radio. Not just any radio, but one made of silver and polished mahogany. There was no mistaking the beautiful object. It was the same one that she had worked on a few weeks before.

His "Ah ha!" made her jump to her feet. He looked up at her curiously. "I just found the pen I was looking for," and he leaned forward to scribble a few lines on a piece of paper. When he was done he handed it to her. "This should do it. I wish you well on your harvest."

"Thank you, Commandant." She glanced at the sheet of paper and folded it and tucked it into her pocket. She turned to leave and then turned back around and, with nerve that she didn't know she had, pointed toward his desk and said, "That's a lovely radio. I've never seen anything like it."

"And you won't again because it was commissioned a couple of years ago for my 30th birthday by a family friend."

Nettie arched her eyebrows. She had thought the lined face belonged to a man in his forties, not to one who apparently was her own age. She unconsciously stroked her own cheek, wondering if the war had had the same effects on her.

Mistaking her silence for interest in the radio, he continued "It is wonderful, isn't it? I was so worried when I got here because when I unpacked it, it wouldn't work. I was so upset, but Frederick saved the day."

"How did he do that?"

"He took it with him and brought it back fixed a few days later. I don't know what I would do without Frederick."

Indeed! She thought. She excused herself, claiming that she had to get back to work.

"Oh, Mademoiselle Dupre," he called as she had just reached the half open door.

"Yes," she said as she paused with her hand on the knob.

"Have you heard from the Colliers or the Klein sisters? No one seems to know where they are."

The hairs on her neck stuck straight up as she turned back around and looked him in the eyes and honestly replied, "No, Herr Commandant, I have not heard from them."

"That's too bad. It was nice to have civilians that spoke German so well."

"Well, unless you allow me to travel to Vichy, you always have me," Nettie said, half-hoping he would mention that she would be allow to leave Blanc Fleur.

"Then I guess I will always have you," he answered emphatically and then added, "I will see you later Mademoiselle Dupre."

I'm sure you will, Nettie said to herself as she left the room.

On the way down the stairs she ran into Frederick who was on his way up. Nettie whispered that she wanted to see him the next day and could he come to the schoolroom at 3:15 the next afternoon? Without looking at her, he answered that he would and continued on his way.

The next day, Nettie stayed behind after the 3 o'clock dismissal bell and washed the blackboard. At promptly a quarter after the hour a knock came on the door and Frederick poked his head around the open door.

"Come in, Frederick," she greeted him with a smile. She then went to the teacher's closet and pulled out a small wooden box that she had brought into town that morning. She opened it and showed him the contents. "I have three jars of honey and these." She unwrapped a small package and showed him a half-dozen beeswax tapers.

He reached into his pocket to pull out his wallet, but Nettie stopped him.

"You don't owe me anything, Frederick."

"I really need to pay you for the honey, the candles, for fix…"

She interrupted him. "No, you don't owe me anything. Just take them." and handed him the box. "By the way how did you know…how did you know about where to leave the radio?"

"I have my secrets, Nettie, as you have yours. And then there are those we have together…"

Nettie blanched at those words. "How is he? As a Commandant, I mean."

Frederick thought for a moment before answering. "He hasn't threatened or beaten me yet. Not even when I spilled coffee in his lap."

Nettie was horrified. "Frederick, you didn't!"

"Trust me, spilling coffee in a man's lap brings out the real person inside," he laughed slyly.

"What was that person like that you brought out?"

Frederick cocked his head to the side and thought again before saying, "Controlled. Very controlled." With that comment he turned around and walked to the door where he turned around and said quietly, "You don't owe me anything, Nett." He then exited and Nettie listened to the echoing sounds of his boots walking quickly down the hall.

She looked out the window overlooking the courtyard and watched Frederick leave the building and make his way back to Headquarters and said softly to herself, "No, Frederick, I owe you everything."

Chapter 9

Dawn had just broken and the ground was still wet with dew when the group of seventy-six assembled in the clearing of the Dupre Orchard. They milled around, awaiting their work orders. Eulalie Dupre, with the help of a few helping hands, stood in the bed of a dray that was hitched to a fine pair of draft horses that belonged to Mousier Mailliez, Anna and Adele's father.

"If I could have your attention!" she shouted through an old homemade megaphone. "May I…"

"We heard you the first time, Mother!" shouted Nettie as everyone quieted down.

Her mother continued, "OK then, here is how today is going to run. Each of you is to take a bag and in small groups, pick your tree clean. When you have completed your picking, you are to make your way back to the clearing and sort the apples into two piles. The better apples go into the bushel baskets here on the ground. The not–so–great apples go into one of the drays. As the drays fill up, they will go to the Roque farm and be made into cider. We have already taken your containers to their farm and you may pick your cider up in the next few days. I hope this year everyone clearly marked their containers to avoid the confusion we had last year." She gave a long look in the direction of several in the crowd. "OK...let's begin."

"Wow, Nett, I thought you were the only bossy one in your family," teased Francois.

Nett gave him a mock dirty look and snipped, "Shut-up, Francois."

From behind them Marie-Claire admonished, "Shhhh. There are children here. We teachers must set an example."

"Just relax, Marie," said a voice further back in the crowd.

"Who was that?" quizzed Nettie.

Marie-Claire blushed, "Mother Superior."

Nettie laughed as she picked up a canvas bag and slipped the handle over her head and picked up a ladder. She followed Margarethe, her husband, and two teenaged sons into the orchard. The boys climbed the stately, old tree and picked the upper branches while their parents picked what they could reach from the ground. Nettie climbed the ladder and picked the areas in between. As their bags filled they made their way back to the clearing and dutifully separated the fruit. The drays made several trips on the old road that led to the back of the orchard. The old road emptied onto a wide, flat road that ran parallel to the stone wall surrounding the orchard. Just a mile further on, the drays would pull into the Roque orchard where waiting workers would run the apples through the press that serviced several orchards in the area.

It was late morning when Eulalie Dupre came looking for her daughter. "Nettie, would you go to the house and tell Nana to start bringing out the food?"

Weary of several hours of picking apples, Nettie was relieved to do something else. She climbed down the ladder and made her way down the path to the farmhouse. The kitchen was humming with activity. Nana and several older women were busy stirring the contents of pans on the stove and mixing things up in big bowls on the kitchen table. Nettie informed her grandmother that it was time to bring the food to the clearing, which caused the ladies to work even faster. In a few minutes, the covered dishes were placed in a hand cart that Nettie pushed slowly over the rutted path to the clearing with the ladies walking behind her carrying the items that wouldn't fit in the cart.

They found that the workers had already laid out their blankets for the picnic and were ready to eat. They placed the dishes along the sides of the wells and cisterns and everyone served themselves. After everyone had stuffed themselves, the adults snoozed under the trees and the children played among the trees.

Nettie laid on her back, her head resting on her hands, which were clasped together. Next to her, Marie-Claire lay in the same position. Comfortable in their silence, they were each lost in their own thoughts when Marie-Claire spoke up. "You know what I like about lying under trees?"

Nettie couldn't imagine. "What, Marie?"

"I like the fact I can look up and see the whole sky. I mean, I can actually see only part of the sky, because of the leaves and branches. Which is OK because the leaves and branches filter out the sun, so I can look up at the sky. My mind fills in the rest of the sky. Does that make sense, Nett?"

"Hmmm. Yes. But why don't you just go to a clearing and look up?"

"You would be blinded by the sun and not see anything at all."

"I guess you're right, but I would like to see the entire sky, the *real* sky without the leaves getting in the way."

After a moment of silence Marie-Claire spoke again. "Nett, the Klein sisters made it to Switzerland."

Nettie sat bolt upright. "Are you serious?"

"Yes. Of course."

"How do you know?"

"I found out. Someone told me."

"Well then, why don't you tell me?" Nettie insisted.

Marie-Claire looked up into the filtered sunshine and replied, "Remember Nett, it's safer to see the sky from under a tree than from a clearing."

Before Nettie could respond, her mother was calling them back to work.

Chapter 10

"OK, everyone back to work!" repeated Eulalie Dupre, interrupting the peace and quiet of the noon hour. After much groaning and yawning, everyone got to their feet and made their way back to the trees they were picking when the call announcing lunch had been heard.

This time Nettie followed Anna and her younger sister Adele to a tree that lined the back stone wall, next to the back entrance. Adele volunteered to climb the tree while the other two picked from the ground. Adele had just settled into her perch when she could be heard saying, "Uh, oh."

"What's wrong?" queried her sister.

"I see something coming down the road," she answered, maneuvering around the upper branches to get a better look.

"Adele! Be careful!" warned Anna. "Is it father with the dray?"

"No, it's a car. A big, black car. I could be wrong but it looks like the Commandant's car."

"Oh not today," moaned Nettie.

They heard a car engine rumbling down the back road. Before it reached the back entrance to the orchard, they heard the engine cut off.

Adele started her commentary. "They are getting out. Yep, it's the Commandant and Frederick along with someone else who is driving. The Commandant and Frederick are walking this way. They just reached the back gate." At this point Adele slid down from her perch and landed next to her sister, who helped her to her feet.

Nettie and Anna turned their eyes to the back entrance just in time to see the Commandant and Frederick walking toward them. To their surprise they were both dressed in old work pants and shirts. The other soldier had apparently stayed behind with the car, as he did not make an appearance.

"What a fine day for picking," enthused the Commandant. "I was wondering if you needed some help." Frederick flashed the group a sympathetic look from behind the back of his master.

No one said anything, a mixture of fear and surprise of seeing him running through his or her minds. Nettie spoke up first. "We don't need any help, but you are welcome to pick as much as you would like."

"I am sure my men would enjoy such a treat. Where do we start?"

Nettie motioned for them to follow her and she led them to the clearing where she gave each a bag and several bushel baskets. The Commandant, ever the meeter and greeter, called each of the people he recognized by name and those he had not met before that day, stopped and chatted with. The civilians, for their part, answered him with friendly indifference and tried not to gape at the sight of the Commandant in faded jeans and frayed work shirt. Nettie hid her impatience at having to wait for him to finish his visitation before leading him and Frederick to a tree that stood in an area that had not already been picked. Nettie dropped the ladder she had carried for them and suggested that they may wish to start picking there.

"Guten Abends, Fraulein Farve," the Commandant called to Clea, who was picking fruit a few trees away. He then spotted a young woman standing on the other side of the tree from Clea and he went to investigate. Nettie rolled her eyes and followed after him.

He approached the brown-eyed blonde, and with his best smile, held out his hand and said, "I don't believe that we have met."

She smiled and took his hand and replied, "Why yes, Herr Commandant, we have met on a couple of occasions. I guess I failed to make an impression."

He looked over the young woman dressed in worn men's clothing and said, "I *know* I would have remembered *you*."

"Hi Sister!" some children cried as they raced past in a game of tag.

His face flushed as the look of realization crossed his features. His shoulders relaxed as a low laugh rang out. He clasped her hand in both of his and said, "I stand corrected, we have indeed met before. And it is a pleasure to met again, Sister Marie-Claire."

Marie-Claire, turning rather pink herself, gave him her best smile.

"I can assure you the nuns never dressed so casually at the school I attended as a boy. Does your Mother Superior know you're out running around like this?"

"Why don't you ask her? She is picking over there. The woman in the red work pants," she teased back.

The Commandant, his face still rather pink, gave a wan smile and released her hand. "I must leave you to your picking, Sister, and start mine while the sun still shines." With that he turned and walked back to the tree that Frederick had already started picking.

Clea poked Marie-Claire in the ribs and whispered in her ear. "He is quite a catch Marie, you may want to rethink this nun thing."

Marie-Claire just tossed her head and went back to work.

Nettie followed the Commandant back to the tree he was working on and decided it might be prudent to stay and keep an eye on the Germans.

"These are lovely apples," said the Commandant, holding an apple up and admiring it. He then took a bite and Nettie watched as his face screwed up. "These are certainly different apples."

Nettie was momentarily horrified when she realized that he had been expecting to bite into a regular apple. She quickly spoke up, "These are apples that we use to produce Calavados brandy. They are more… ah…tart than most apples."

"You can say that again! What are these people going to do with them? Surely not eat them."

"Most will be made into cider. The rest will be dried, made into apple butter, pies. But yes, some will be eaten raw. When one is hungry, food is food."

He looked rather taken aback, but said nothing.

Nettie squirmed uncomfortably. "I'm sorry, I should have warned you and saved you all the trouble you have gone through."

"Nonsense. I will just take them to the cider press and have them made into cider. My men will be most pleased." He then invited Nettie to pick with him and Frederick.

Seeing no graceful way of getting out of that, she agreed and worked with them for the afternoon.

It was not until she heard her Mother and Nana saying their good-byes to some of their friends that Nettie took the opportunity to excuse herself to do the same.

Between bidding people farewell, Nana leaned over and whispered in Nettie's ear, "Who is that handsome young man with Frederick?"

Nettie snorted, "That is no handsome young man Nana, that is the new Commandant I was telling you about. You really should get into town more often."

"Why is the Commandant dressed like that picking *our* apples?" she quizzed her granddaughter.

"He said he wanted a treat for his men. What could I say?" Then she laughed as she relayed what had happened when he tasted one of the fruits and added, "He's going to take them to the press and have cider made instead."

"Is that the real reason he is here, Nett?" Nana pressed.

Uneasily, Nettie told her about his interest in who had been there that day, especially those he had not met before, or in Marie-Claire's case, those he had not recognized.

"This must be your Nana," came a voice from behind them.

Nettie shot her grandmother a look of "See what I mean?"

The Commandant inquired of her recent birthday and thanked her for the opportunity to join in the apple harvest before asking where he could wash up.

Nettie led him to the clearing and pulled up a bucket of cold, fresh water and poured it into a large ceramic bowl. He rolled up his sleeves and unbuttoned two more buttons of his shirt before dipping his hands into the bowl and splashing his face, neck and forearms. When he was done, Nettie handed him a towel from a pile that had been placed on the side of the well. As his face was buried in the towel, Nettie looked up and noticed Clea in the shadows of a tree, leaning against its trunk, watching the entire scene play out before her. Seeing Nettie frowning at her, she turned and walked away.

As the Commandant put the towel on the side of the well he said, "You have a lovely Orchard. Would it be possible to have a tour of it?"

Nettie, after a long day of picking, had hoped he would make a swift departure. Seeing no alternative, she replied that she would be most happy to.

She began, "I guess we can start right here. As you can see, these are our wells and cisterns. The local legend says that the Maid of Orleans herself was here and at the request of the farmer who owned this land, thrust her sword into the soil and moments later water sprung up and has fed these fields and orchards ever since."

"Are you speaking of Joan of Arc? I didn't realize she was associated with this area or specialized in ground water," he added rather cheekily.

Nettie found herself smiling in spite of herself. "They are artesian wells and whether St. Joan had anything to do with them I don't know, but it does make for a nice story. But she is connected with Normandy.

She was tried for heresy and witchcraft and burned at the stake in Rouen in 1431."

"She is the national heroine of France, I understand."

"Yes, she has been for centuries, although she was canonized by the Church just recently, in 1934."

"Please tell me more about Normandy as you show me around your farm, Mademoiselle."

She motioned for him to follow her and he quickly stepped to her side, his arm brushing hers as they made their way down the narrow path to the farmhouse. She continued the conversation with "France has been settled by several different peoples. Among the first were the Celts. One of the Celtic tribes was known as Gallia, which is why France was known as Gaul in ancient times. The Romans were next and their ruins of theaters, baths, and other buildings can still be found all around France. Next came the Franks, Germans really, who did something right when they drove the invaders from North Africa out and saved the European continent from becoming an Islamic state."

"I'm glad to hear that Germans did something good," the Commandant offered.

Nettie shrugged and continued, "One of the last of the Frankish kings was Charlemagne. While he did many great things in his lifetime, when he died his kingdom was divided up in several pieces and has caused wars ever since. For example, Germany and France have fought over the Alsace-Lorraine region, where my father was from, ever since."

"Yes, you did make it quite clear that you consider yourself French and not half German," the Commandant stated.

"Just as the Germans' occupation of Alsace from time to time never made his family any less French, just as now the Germans being here now makes *me* any less French."

He stopped and turned toward her. Nettie took an uneasy step backwards as he tipped her chin up, forcing her to look at him as he said, "I didn't come to argue with you, I just wanted to learn more about your country."

"Yes, I am sorry, Commandant," she whispered.

He dropped his hand and said heartily, "Please go on with your history lesson. Why is this region called Normandy?"

Nettie swallowed nervously and continued with "The next invaders were from Norway, Sweden, and Denmark. These were Vikings or sometimes referred to as Norsemen. They besieged this area and settled here in northwestern France and it came to be known as Normandy. William the Conqueror, who invaded England in 1066, was the Duke of Normandy. His descendants would claim parts of France and that would lead to more wars."

"I guess people never tire of wars," the Commandant commented as he shook his head sadly.

Nettie shrugged, and deciding to change the subject, pointed out the house, the outbuildings, garden, and chicken coop.

He pointed toward several white wooden boxes stacked in the back yard. "Are those bee hives?"

Nettie responded in the affirmative.

He advanced toward them while Nettie walked nervously behind him. "Is this where my predecessor met his unfortunate end?"

"Yes," was all Nettie would say.

A few bees hummed lazily around his head and one landed on his shoulder and crawled around for a moment before taking flight again. He looked the area over and commented, "They seem docile enough."

"He fell and landed on their hives. They were instinctively protecting themselves," Nettie hastily added.

"Indeed," he said, glancing at Nettie.

She motioned him away from the hives with, "Come, I have much more to show you before it gets too dark to see anything."

Hoping to prevent him from asking any questions about the bees or the demise of the previous Commandant, Nettie forced herself to chat away as she led him back down the path towards the distillery. Forcing open one of the large, wooden doors she motioned him inside and continued her chatter. "This is our distillery. As you know, this area of Normandy is known as the Calvados region because of the apple brandy that is produced only here in this part of the world. Normally we would have at least two stills producing brandy this time of year, but as you can see, we cleaned all the equipment and stored everything on these shelves."

The Commandant looked with genuine interest at the wooden shelves lining the building and the barrels stacked everywhere. "Are any of these barrels full?" he asked somewhat hopefully.

Nettie sobered, "No. My brother sold off the entire inventory soon after the Germans arrived here in Blanc Fleur. He…ah…disappeared soon after. The three of us can barely handle keeping up the garden and orchard. We don't have time to produce the brandy. Plus the Germans…" She stopped herself in time.

"Might help themselves?" the Commandant finished for her.

"Yes," she replied softly.

"That is too bad. I really wanted to try some while I was stationed here."

"I am sure you can find some at other orchards. Some have been able to continue operation, at least on a smaller scale." She cocked her head and asked, "Are you to be stationed elsewhere?"

He looked surprised and then stumbled, "I don't know…I'm here until my work is done…until the war ends…I guess."

Nettie looked at him curiously; she found it an odd answer.

Turning on his heels he exited the building with Nettie following behind. He motioned to the trees and asked, "You still have a lot of fruit on the trees, will it be allowed to rot?"

"No. Mother, Nana, and I will pick what we want. Then while I am at work they get to do the drying, hauling to the cider mill, and make applesauce, apple butter and other things out of them. Mr. Roquert, the man who owns the cider mill, will come with his family and pick the rest. He will make it into cider and sell it in neighboring villages. Nothing will be wasted," she assured him.

He picked an apple from a tree and bit into it. "I bet that apple sauce packs quite a punch," he said as he screwed up his face at the rather bitter taste.

"I would be most happy to bring you some," she offered.

"I would be happy to try some. How long has your family owned the orchard?"

"My mother's family has owned the land for generations. They raised crops and dairy cattle. But it was her grandparents that planted the trees and built the original distillery, which was torn down years ago."

"How did your father come to live here in Normandy? I mean, all the way from Alsace."

"My father was a traveling salesman. He sold equipment used in the production of liqueur and he paid a sales call to the farmhouse. The rest, as they say, is history."

"Will you inherit the farm someday?"

Nettie shrugged. "I suppose so."

The Commandant looked at her out of the corner of his eye and made no further comment on the subject. "So, if I were to have the opportunity to travel around Normandy, what do you suggest that I see?"

Nettie noticeably brightened, thinking about her home providence. Thoughtfully she Answered, "Mont Saint-Michel. It's a tiny, cone-shaped island, just off the coast of Normandy, near Avranches. It is capped off with a thirteenth century Benedictine Abby. It is considered to be one of the best examples of Gothic architecture anywhere in the world."

"That sounds interesting. Where else should I visit?"

"Well, you could go to Villequier where Leopoldine, the favorite daughter of Victor Hugo, died along with her young husband in a boating accident. They are buried at the small church there."

"Hmmm, maybe some place more cheerful," he mused. Nettie went on to describe a few other areas of local interest as they made their way through the trees and after reaching the back wall, headed toward the back entrance. Nettie was surprised to find herself relaxing and actually enjoying sharing with this man the beauty of her homeland. "And since you were educated by nuns, maybe you remember Saint Terese who was born in Alencon and entered the Convent of Lisieux which is not far from here. She was also called the 'Little Flower.'"

The Commandant nodded, "Ah yes, she wrote her autobiography that I read years ago. I especially remember that she had taken as her motto the words 'Love is repaid by love alone.'"

"My sister was named for her…" added Nettie, her smile fading. The Commandant reached out and gently squeezed her arm but said nothing. Taken by surprise, Nettie didn't pull away from his touch, but did pick up her pace to the back entrance of the orchard.

Frederick and the driver had parked the car at the back entrance and were waiting patiently for the Commandant to return. Seeing him, they informed him that they had delivered the apples to the press and would pick up the cider there the next day. Nettie pointed to a small herd of cattle standing in the field opposite where they were standing and told him that was where the original dairy had stood.

"Don't you still own the cattle?"

"Well, no. Not anymore." She went on to explain that the cattle had been sold to a neighboring farm when her father died. "My sister and I would work there in exchange for milk and beef until…until she left," she finished lamely before changing the subject by pointing to the hedgerows that framed the field in which the cattle were grazing. "Another unique feature found here in Normandy are the hedgerows that surround the farmers' fields. In French they are called 'bocages' and trust me, you don't want to try to go through one because you will get all cut up by the branches, if you could get through one at all. They are stronger than they may look from a distance."

"I will take your advice and stay out of the bocages." He smiled softly at her before continuing, "It's a wonderful farm. I hope someday it will come back to what it was. I have something for you. Just a small thank-you for your hospitality and apples." He led the way to his car and opened the back door and reached in and pulled out a twenty-pound bag of white sugar and placed it in her hands.

"Why, thank you," was all she could stammer. Such a gift was indeed generous during this time of shortages.

"Can you carry that? Come, get in, and we will drive you to the house."

"I can carry it," she assured him.

The soldiers got into the car and the driver started the motor and put it into gear and drove down the back road toward town. She stood there watching them disappear, hugging the precious sugar to her. She was relived that the day had gone well and even more relieved that he was gone. Gone for now anyway. But in the back of her mind was the nagging question of why had he come in the first place. He couldn't be that desperate for a few bushels of tart apples. He hadn't fooled her, he had been bothered when he had not recognized Marie-Claire and relieved when he found out who she was. Why? Her arms ached by the time she reached the side door to the kitchen and let herself in. A cold supper was set on the table as her mother and Nana had already gone to bed, exhausted by the long day. Nettie sat at the table in semi-darkness and ate and before the sun had completely set, she went upstairs, removed her shoes, lay down on the bed and slept soundly until morning.

Chapter 11

September brought with it shorter and cooler days. The school, faced with a lack of heating fuel and the ever-present curfew, changed the hours of the school day. Classes would start at 9 o'clock and the dismissal bell would ring at 2 o'clock. While teacher and student alike disliked the shortened hours, they knew that when the winds of winter blew the hardest, school would be out until spring. Nettie longed for the days when school was out for the summer and she could work on the farm. Now she worked during the summer and had the long, dark winter months free when there was little work to be done. Then again, the world was upside down, why not the school as well.

On one of those crisp September mornings, nearly two weeks after the apple harvest, Nettie rode her bicycle into town. As usual she rode past the Commandant on her way to the library. It was like clockwork now. The smile, tip of the cap from him, and the briefest of smiles and greetings from her. And going to work wasn't the only time he appeared. Shopping, visiting a café with friends, pretty much anywhere she went in public, he would be right behind her. The change in the start of school had only confused him for one day. She had overheard Frederick politely inform Mr. LaPierre that the Commandant wished to be informed of any change of the school day, to afford the greatest amount of protection to the students and staff. After Frederick had returned to Headquarters, Mr. LaPierre had openly wondered what the Germans were protecting them *from*.

She stepped off her bicycle and led it to the gate beside the library. She was surprised to find it ajar. She pushed it the rest of the way open and was about to pull the bicycle through the gate when she came face to face with Clea who had stepped out of the garden. Clea grabbed the handlebars and pulled the bicycle through the gate and leaned it against the wall of the library and then reached over and shut the gate behind them.

"Nett, I have an idea. I know you will think that I am mad, but perhaps I can help," she whispered excitedly.

"What is it?" Nettie asked warily.

"Well, you know Rolfe seems to be glued to your side." At this observation Nettie blanched. It was true, even people from the distant farms seemed to be aware of the Commandant's interest in Bernadette Dupre. This especially concerned her. Although some French civilians cultivated both personal and business relationships with the occupying Germans, Nettie knew very well the connotation connected with a single French woman and a German Commandant. She had tried her best to avoid him. It seemed that she spent half her time looking over her shoulder. It was to no avail, as he appeared everywhere with no warning.

"…I thought I could get him interested in me, if, of course, you don't really want him," Clea finished.

"I'm sorry, what did you say?"

"Nett! Do I have to repeat myself?" When it became obvious that she would, she repeated, "I thought we could have a party or better yet, a Sunday dinner and I could make a few…ah.moves. He would see that you don't care a lick for him and he would find me much more fascinating. Sort of like the saying 'one in the hand is like two in the bush.'"

"You *have* gone mad! Besides even you must realize the real reason he finds me so *interesting* in the first place."

Clea tossed her head. "Think of me as the person who jumps off the sidelines to distract the bull just before he gores the matador."

Giving her friend a long look, Nettie warned, "Are you sure you wish to do that?"

Clea dismissed the question with a wave of her hand and with a sly wink added, "He'll be a bullock in no time."

"Does your mother know you talk like this?" Nettie laughed before she dissolved into tears. "Oh Clea! I don't know what to do. Everywhere I go, there he is, smiling, helpful. He never really goes away."

Clea put her arm around her. "It's OK. Maybe this will help."

They opened the gate and walked together to the school. While they walked, Clea laid out her plan. "Here is what we will do. We invite him to Sunday dinner. I flirt, toss *my beautiful* blonde hair. And then he will be mine," she said matter-of-factly.

"You mean he will be your problem. Are you sure that is what you want?" stated Nettie.

"No…Yes…No. It will be fine for me," assured Clea. She turned her head, the matter was finished as far as she was concerned, and nothing more needed to be said or explained.

When they reached the steps of the school, they heard, "Guten Morgan, Mademoiselle Dupre…Farve." They politely waved at the Commandant who was sitting on the steps of the German Headquarters, casually smoking a cigarette.

Nettie grabbed Clea's arm and whispered, "OK, let's do it."

Clea answered with a nod of her head and said, "I'll make up the guest list. Those from school will make up most of the list. We'll have it at my house because it's easiest to get to. Plus it's across the street from his house so he won't feel rushed to get home. Let's see. Today is Thursday, we can hold it the Sunday after next."

"Thanks, Clea," a relieved Nettie replied. At this point she was willing to try anything.

The selected Sunday dawned chilly and overcast, which reflected Nettie's demeanor. She stood in the Farve's dining room with her hands on her hips looking over the table set with the finest linen, china, and silverware. She had to admit that Mrs. Farve, the widow of the town's former physician, had wonderful taste and Clea seemed to have inherited the same fine taste, except for her taste in men. She could hear her mother and Nana in the kitchen with Mrs. Farve preparing the meal. They were expecting twenty people and were taking great delight in the occasion since they rarely had anything to celebrate these days. Clea and Nettie had struggled for a reason why they were holding this dinner party. They had given a vague but practical answer of wanting to celebrate the fine harvest that summer.

A knock came at the door. It was Anna and Adele who had walked in from their farm and were coming to pick up their friends for church. "Come on, Clea," called Nettie from the bottom of the stairs as she grabbed her coat. Clea ran down the steps. It had taken her forever to get ready but it was evident that the extra care had paid off. Her hair was done up in a dramatic French twist. The cornflower blue eyes were enhanced by the gray wool suit she wore and the slightest touch of make-up that was required of one of such natural beauty. The older women had decided to stay behind and bid the younger people to attend Mass without them.

"We'll be late if we don't hurry," chided Adele. The four women hurried out the door with Clea donning an attractive black beret with black feathers tucked into a silver brooch that was pinned at a rather jaunty angle. They had only gone a few yards when they were hailed from a side street.

Without even bothering to look, Nettie muttered "I thought he would meet us there."

"More time for us to talk," smiled Clea as she made a grand gesture in waving to him and then trotted ahead of the others to meet him halfway. When she reached his side, she slipped her hand under his unoffered arm. She looked up at him and smiled "I am so glad we have a chance to walk together to church."

If he was surprised by her actions, he did not show it. He smiled warmly at her and let her lead him down the road while the others followed closely behind. Clea immediately engaged him in conversation. "I like Father Bolet so much more than Father Girard. Father Girard always mumbled his way through Mass. Half the time I was giving responses at the wrong time." The rest of the female members of the group snickered. She gave the wrong response because her attention was usually focused on the single men of the parish.

"I guess I am at a loss, since I arrived after this Father Girard…" started the Commandant.

"Died," piped up Adele as she moved up to walk next to him.

He continued, "Your Father Bolet seems quite good, very much in tune with his parish. I am hoping that I may have such a relationship with this town."

The women exchanged quick glances with each other. Without missing a beat Anna jumped in with, "Oh he *is* so much better. Remember when Father Girard was performing Chloe Choquet's funeral and he kept referring to her as 'Martine'? Who was Martine anyway?" Everyone joined in with her infectious deep laugh.

Nettie was relieved when they reached St. Mary's, the town's only church. Being forced to stop talking came as a relief to her. That relief was short lived as the Commandant maneuvered himself as to sit between Nettie and Anna, with Clea on the other side of Anna. Nettie proceeded to spend the next hour trying to edge away from him and being rewarded with sharp jabs in the ribs from Adele who wanted her seat to herself, thank you. Every muscle in her body seemed tense. Every fiber of her being wanted to get away from him. They were clustered so tightly in the pew that she felt his body heat and smelled his expensive cologne. She fantasized about getting up and leaving, but what would she say? What would he think? Besides he would probably just follow her out. She was so flustered that she found herself singing out of sync with the rest of the congregation, causing Adele to flash curious looks her way. After what seemed an eternity, the Mass ended and Nettie nearly trampled Adele in trying to exit the pew. As they walked back to the Farve residence, Nettie walked ten paces behind the others. She was still trying to calm herself down. The Commandant did not seem to notice as Clea hung on one arm and the others kept up a lively chatter without any need for Nettie to join in, much to her relief.

When they reached the Farve household, Clea led the group inside, not that the racket they had made hadn't already announced their arrival. They sat around the spacious front room with a roaring fire in the hearth and they waited for the rest of the guests to arrive. Simple hors d'oeuvres and apple cider were passed around as everyone kept up a steady conversation. Every few minutes a knock would come at the door and an invited guest or two would join in the party. Nettie found herself relaxing. The food was fabulous, the fire welcoming and soothing. Everything was going well. The Commandant was sitting in an overstuffed chair by the window with Clea sitting on the matching ottoman looking at him like an adoring puppy. She wondered if she was the only one who noticed that he seemed to be keeping his left hand, the one with the simple gold band, in sight at all times.

After smelling the delicious aroma wafting from the kitchen for what seemed like forever, Nana announced that dinner was ready and for everyone to take their seats. They gave the head of the table to Mrs. Farve with Clea to her left with the Commandant next to her. Nana sat to the right of Mrs. Farve with Nettie next to her and across from the Commandant, which seemed to please him. They had placed Nettie's mother at the foot of the table because it was nearest the kitchen and she would act as server. They had made sure that Frederick, the only other German invited, was sitting down at the other end of the table next to Eulalie Dupre.

The meal proved to be more delicious than it smelled. Anna and Adele had donated the three chickens, with everyone else providing either a side dish or a dessert. The conversation was lively and eventually got around to the topic of what books everyone had been reading recently.

"What have you read recently, Herr Commandant?" asked Adele who was sitting to his left.

"I hate to admit it but the last book I read was 'Little Women.'" At this Adele shrieked with laughter. Clea couldn't resist asking, "Why on earth were you reading that! Surely the public library has other books on its shelves."

He blushed slightly. "Actually, I came across a volume on my travels and before I mailed it to my daughter, I read it. Rather desperate for a good read, I suppose."

"Did you enjoy it?" inquired Nettie politely.

"Yes, but the parts where the one sister dies and the other chops her hair off were rather depressing."

"Do you equate those actions?" asked Nettie.

A sharp look from her mother at the other end of the table warned Nettie to let the matter drop. The Commandant let the question go by and engaged in a discourse of the book with Adele who, it turned out, had just read it last year. Nettie toyed with her food, shoveling the mashed potatoes around to admire the roses that were painted on the china plate. For some reason she glanced up to find that the Commandant was turning a dark shade of red, the gray eyes smoldering embers. At first she thought he was choking on his food, but quickly realized that something else was horribly amiss. Clea was calmly chatting up a storm; her shoulder was leaning against his. Nettie let her eyes follow Clea's arm downward where, even though hidden by the table, seemed to end…Good grief! Nettie sucked in her breath as the realization of what Clea was doing hit her. Her eyes shot up to the storm-filled eyes in front of her and instinctively her foot shot out in the hopes it would reach Clea. It must have found its mark because the face before her returned to its normal pale complexion. Horrified, she spent the rest of the meal staring down at her plate and noticed that the Commandant also finished his meal in silence. As soon as possible, Nettie claimed she was full and would help with the dishes so that those who cooked could now relax. She cleared the table as the others made their way back to the front room. Nettie was starting to wash the dishes when Nana came into the kitchen.

"Nettie," she scolded, "you need to get out there with your guests."

Nettie was near tears at the thought of what had just transpired in front of her during dinner. "Please Nana, I'd rather stay here."

Nana touched her elbow and whispered in her ear, "We will talk about this later. Get out there and make sure everything is OK." Nettie nodded her head and walked out to the front room. To her relief everyone was still there. The Commandant was once again seated in the overstuffed chair by the window, but now Adele occupied the ottoman, and his attention. Clea sat in a rocking chair on the other side of the room and was talking with Francois and Cat. Nettie herself found a seat on the davenport and joined in quiet conversation with Frederick and Margarethe.

The mantle clock struck four o'clock and those living out of town, including the Dupres, stood up and made their good-byes. They would have to hurry to make it home before darkness fell. The Commandant wished them a good evening as he himself got up from his chair and, claiming a busy schedule for the next day, said good-night. Anna and Adele would walk as far as the cut off that led to their farm with Nettie and her family. Nettie walked in silence ahead of the small group, trying to block out the whispered conversation going on behind her back. She was uncertain if she should be embarrassed or just frightened about the events of that day, so she settled for both.

As soon as they reached their home, Nettie made her excuses and went up to her bedroom straight away. She threw herself on her bed, pressing her face in the mattress, trying to block out the scene of his angry face staring into hers. What would he do to them? He was probably at Headquarters thinking of something right now. She hid her face in her arms and wanted to cry, but the deep fear inside her would not let the tears come. Eventually she fell into a fitful sleep.

A few hours later she woke up with a start. She looked at the ticking clock on the nightstand and it read 10 o'clock. Was that all it was? She shook off her drowsiness and got to her feet and looked out the window. She could see the shadows created by the apple trees by the light of the moon. The shadows were thinning as some of the leaves had begun to fall in earnest from their branches. For some reason the trees and the shadows frightened her. She shivered, and crossing her arms, hugged her arms closer, trying to warm and calm herself. Why had they become so frightening, so suddenly unfamiliar to her? She had grown up under those branches. She turned away and decided she needed a drink of water to clear her mind and made her way down stairs.

She was surprised to find Nana sitting at the table in the dark.

"Are you all right, Nana?" asked Nettie hesitantly.

"We need to talk, Nett," she answered in a straightforward manner as she arose to put the kettle on for some coffee.

Nettie sat down across from her grandmother, dreading what was coming.

Nana sat back down and looked at her in the eyes and said, "What the hell was going on during dinner?" Nettie had to admit that Nana was not one for beating around the bush.

"We are having a pleasant meal and suddenly Clea is…ah…doing *that* to the Commandant *at* the dinner table no less! I haven't always approved of her, but this time she went too far. I am upset, no, *disappointed* that you didn't seem at all surprised at what she did. What is going on Nett? Do you want to be dragged into Headquarters again?"

"I know. I should have refused when she offered to flirt with him. I had no idea she was going to do *that* however! But Nana, everywhere I go, there he is. I was, no, I *am* that desperate." Her voice faltered.

Nana poured each a cup of steaming coffee and sat down. "It is obvious that she was doing it for you. She is a true friend, but that stunt was dangerous." She took a few sips and continued, "That's the problem, he is chasing you and you are the one looking over your shoulder. If you spend all your time doing that, then you can't see where *you're* going. Do you understand, Nett?"

"So I should do what?" she asked.

"Let him catch you, in a way of speaking. Make it appear that you are going out of your way to see and talk to him. Then *he* will be the one looking over his shoulder."

Nettie gave a half smile. "But he has nothing to hide, unlike me."

"Doesn't he? Maybe he does, maybe he doesn't. But Nett, this town is just too small for you to hide in. You just make yourself look guilty and you are endangering others."

Nettie clasped her hands around the hot cup of coffee and looked into the dark depths of the steaming liquid. Her grandmother was right, she knew that. She looked up and said to the older woman, "You're right. I will see how things go tomorrow after what happened today. I'll think of some way to become…friends with him."

"Good," said Nana as she patted Nettie's arm. "I think it will make things better for you, for everyone."

Chapter 12

The next morning Nettie awoke with her heart in her throat. They would find out that day what consequences their actions would bring down upon them. It was the usual crowd she passed on the way to the library, with one notable exception, the absence of the Commandant. When she entered the school building she took a detour down the hall of the first floor and looked into the kindergarten classroom. She was relieved to find Clea helping several students pick a spilled box of crayons off the floor. Nettie turned and hurried to the second floor without trying to attract Clea's attention. Marie-Claire had already started class when Nettie slipped into the back door of the classroom. Without missing a beat in her lecture on geography, Marie-Claire nodded toward the back postboard. Nettie turned to find a folded note tacked to it. Visibly shaking, she took out the tack and unfolded the note and read it.

In neat, precise handwriting was the following: "Please come to my office at your earliest convenience. Thank you, Rolfe." She breathed a sigh of relief. Perhaps his signing in such a casual manner meant that they were not in as much trouble as she had feared.

There was no use putting off the inevitable. Nettie waited until Marie-Claire glanced back in her direction and then pointed toward the door to indicate that she was leaving. Marie-Claire nodded and gave her a curious look. Nettie wasn't looking forward to explaining to the young nun why she was being summoned to the Commandant's office. She walked with measured steps across the courtyard, breathing deeply, trying to remain calm. A soldier stationed at a desk inside the door of Headquarters inquired as to what she wanted. She showed him the note and he requested that she follow him upstairs. He knocked on the Commandant's door and after receiving a positive reply he opened the door and motioned for Nettie to enter. She hesitated and he had to motion to her a second time. She slowly walked in and stood just inside the door, forcing the parting soldier to push her out of the way so he could shut the door behind her.

To her surprise, he was not sitting behind the great wooden desk, but in a rocking chair placed next to the window. He stood up and offered her a similar chair next to his. Seeing no option to the offered chair, she walked quickly over to the empty chair and sat down. Nettie sat stiffly in the rocking chair while keeping her eyes locked on the folded hands in her lap. After a moment of awkward silence, he spoke. "After yesterday," Nettie blanched, "I realized I hadn't read most of the books and novels you and the others were discussing. I was wondering if we could start a book club?"

Nettie hoped her look of relief was not too evident. "We? As in me, the other teachers, and you?"

"No, just you and I."

"Oh."

"You could select the material. I am sure you have a better idea of what is worth reading than I do. I thought we could meet on Wednesdays and Saturdays, starting this Wednesday."

Her first instinct was to say no, she was too busy with her job and her chores at home. But she also realized that this was both the solution to her problem and more of a command than an actual request.

"Yes, I'll do it," she forced out of her mouth. "I'll find something that we will both enjoy reading."

"Good," he smiled. "I'll see you after school on Wednesday." With that he started to get to his feet and Nettie followed suit. He had put his hand on the doorknob when she swallowed hard and asked, "Is that all, Herr Commandant?"

"No, there is nothing else." And then he added, "May I call you Bernadette, Mademoiselle Dupre?"

She turned around and faced him with her best smile, before stating, "No. My friends call me Nettie."

"You may call me Rolfe."

During lunch on the steps of the school, she told her friends what the Commandant had asked her to do.

"What will you select? I guess 'Little Women' is out," Francois stated with as straight a face as he could muster.

"Maybe you could discuss the Good Book," suggested Marie-Claire.

"I don't think that is what he has in mind. What about 'Lady Chatterly's Lover'?" suggested Anna, getting into the spirit of the conversation.

"I think that is what Clea had in mind," roared Francois. The others pretended not to understand what he was talking about and Marie-Claire demanded to know what was so funny.

Mr. LaPierre interrupted their laughter, much to Nettie's and Clea's relief. "Here is the fall and winter school schedule." He handed Marie-Claire a sheet of paper and left to inform the rest of the teachers and staff.

Marie-Claire read it aloud to the others clustered around her. "It says that we can make it through November with a five day, 9 a.m. to 2 p.m. schedule. For December we will have classes Monday through

Wednesday 10 a.m. to 2 p.m. We will close the week before Christmas and re-open sometime in March." Marie-Claire folded the sheet and they all looked glumly at each other.

"Well, we all knew it was coming. The schedule is the same as it was the last two years," mumbled Margarethe. The others were silent, each thinking of the coming winter months with little to do and some of them stuck on lonely farms.

"I guess Nettie will be the only one with a pupil after Christmas," teased Francois.

"I would be more than willing to share," she sarcastically offered.

"Oh no. He is all yours!" they laughed.

"Ask him if he needs help with his geography," offered Marie-Claire.

Francois couldn't resist baiting her. "Sure Marie, you can tell him and all his kraut friends where to go."

"That isn't what I meant," she huffed and walked off.

"Francois, you shouldn't be so mean to her," reprimanded Margarethe.

"Look, they've taken over our entire country, our entire lives, in some cases murdered our friends and relatives and you want them to take over my sense of humor? My soul? They'll never get it. Those cowards will have to kill me first. If I ever get the chance to send one of those bastards to hell, I will." Ending his diatribe, he stood up and entered the school.

"Well, this has been a pleasant lunch," commented Anna as she gathered up the remains of her lunch and with the others went back to work.

Nettie remained seated on the steps, her lunch untouched. She rested her chin in her hands and looked across the courtyard. She tried to remember when that building had been just a school building. It had seemed so long ago. Actually, just three years ago, but in a way, a lifetime ago. She envied Marie-Claire and Francois. Marie-Claire still had her kind heart and Francois still gave his biting commentaries. As for herself,

Nettie no longer recognized the pinched face looking back at her in the mirror. She felt hollow, she no longer dared to dream of tomorrow, because she knew that tomorrow might not come for her. For any of them. As she idly looked across the courtyard, the doors swung open and Frederick emerged with the Commandant after him. Seeing her, the Commandant waved. Nettie forced a smile and waved back. She then stood up and grabbed her lunch pail and pushed open the double doors leading back into the school. Later, sitting at the dinner table with her mother and Nana, she told them of the Commandant's request of a book club just for the two of them.

"That sounds like it could be interesting," commented Nana with visible relief.

"You have all those books upstairs. You might as well get some use out of them," added her mother.

After dinner and the chores were completed, Nettie's mother and Nana relaxed downstairs with their sewing projects. Nettie made her way up the stairs and opened the door to her brother's room. The room was pretty much as he had left it nearly three years ago. The bed was still made with the same muslin sheets and wool blankets. The wardrobe still held what clothing he had left behind. His cologne and toiletry items still adorned the dresser. The only change to be found to the room was the abundance of books. Books were everywhere. They lined the shelves in double rows, were stacked under the bed, and were stacked on any available floor space. These were the books that had once lined the bookshelves in her classroom. After France had fallen, in June of 1940, and before the Germans had made their way to their small town, Nettie had brought a few at a time home with her on her bicycle. Other teachers had taken in a small percentage of the collection and a few remained at the school, but the bulk of the collection was stacked around the room. There had been fear that the Germans would burn the school, if not the town, and their delight in book burnings had already been noted. Optimistically, they had all believed the war would be over in a few months and the books would be returned to their rightful place in her classroom. She sighed as she looked at the dusty volumes. Here they had sat for three years. How much longer would they stay stacked in her brother's room? Not that her brother needed the room. Except for a note smuggled to them once in a while, they didn't hear from her brother or sister. Would she ever see them again? Would she still be here if they came back? Shaking off those thoughts she sat down in the midst of the volumes and gently picked up a few volumes and brushed the dust off their leather-bound spines. She smiled as she read the titles and author's names. Memories of the joy she had in reading them, in teaching them, came flooding back. She enjoyed the young children that she taught now, but how she longed to teach literature to older students again. She had always found purpose in introducing the next generation to the people and places she had come to know in the world of books.

What should she introduce the Commandant to? She reached out and picked up a book lying on top of a stack of books. It was the "Odyssey" by Homer. No, that would be too long and he might find that boring. Maybe later, she thought. She next dug into a stack of books by Jane Austen and found "Emma", "Persuasion", and "Sense and Sensibility". No, she decided they dealt with proper society and romance, two things she didn't feel like discussing with *Rolfe. Rolfe*! Just the thought of calling him that made her feel ill. But hopefully it would not be for much longer.

Another pile contained books by the American author Ernest Hemingway. She had copies of "The Sun Also Rises" and "A Farewell To Arms". But remembering they depicted the last war, she turned those down as well. She suddenly remembered that he had published another book at the start of the war, "For Whom The Bell Tolls," she believed the title had been, and she wondered if it was any good. She reached under the bed and pulled out a pile that had been deliberately shoved there and looked at them. They were also by an American, John Steinbeck.

She had the title "Of Mice and Men" and "The Grapes of Wrath". It was then that she remembered why the volumes had been placed out of the way. The later book had caused much controversy because it was believed that the book had "Communist" undertones because of how it portrayed society. She was well aware that the Germans considered the Communists their greatest enemy. It was this very reason that the Communist members of the French Underground were considered the most daring and effective. They had nothing to lose. If caught, they would be executed without pause. Nettie placed the Steinbeck books aside. She would hide them in a much safer area.

Digging into the piles of books once again, Nettie pulled out the perfect book, "Treasure Island," by Robert Louis Stevenson. Yes! No romance, just a bunch of pirates.

It seemed like a good place to start.

Chapter 13

All too quickly Wednesday arrived. The dismissal bell rang promptly at 2 p.m. and Nettie and Marie-Claire helped the children into their coats and walked with them down the stairs.

"I hope things go well," whispered Marie-Claire as they separated in the courtyard.

Nettie gave her friend a half-smile and replied, "I hope so too."

She was waved past the soldier stationed at the desk and walked alone up the stairs. She half hoped he had forgotten and was out for the day. He hadn't, and answered her knock at the door in person. He inquired as to her well being as he ushered her to one of the rocking chairs set next to the windows. After they were both seated, he leaned forward and asked with sincere interest, "What book have you selected?"

She reached into her book bag and pulled out two books and handed one to him. She said with mustered enthusiasm, "I thought we would start with 'Treasure Island.'"

"Oh," was all he said until he opened the book and looked up at her and said, "it's in French."

"Of course." Then she stammered, "I'm sorry, I just assumed that you could read it since you speak it so well."

"I can read the simplest of words, probably not even as well as your fourth graders. I learned to speak French when I was in France the first time and when I was stationed in North Africa."

Nettie gave him a surprised look and asked, "The first time?"

He momentarily appeared flustered before he replied, in a matter of fact way, "In 1940. I served under Rommel and was with him when we invaded France. Then I was assigned to North Africa and served under him there."

Nettie didn't think that she could dislike this man more than she already did, but with the knowledge of his role in the defeat of her country, she did. Rather than making a comment, she opened her copy of the book and said, "I could go ahead and read this story out loud to you and when I get home I will see what books I have that are in German."

"That would be great," he enthused.

Nettie bent her head toward the book in her hands and began, "Squire Trelawney, Dr. Livesy, and the rest of those gentlemen having asked me…"

She read for about a half an hour before she shut the book and they discussed the few chapters she had read aloud. The time went by quickly and it was only when Nettie glanced out the window and noticed that the shadows in the courtyard had lengthened, that she ventured, "It will soon be dark, and I must get home," as she rose from her chair.

"Yes, of course. I didn't realize it was so late. For our session on Saturday, I thought we would meet outdoors and get some fresh air. How does that sound?"

"Sounds nice," answered Nettie, wondering what he had in mind.

"Good. I'll pick you up at 10 o'clock at your farm and we will go to the cliffs."

"The cliffs? I thought they were off limits."

"They are, but I think I can find a place. I'll see you then, if not before."

As it turned out she didn't see him Thursday or Friday. She took this as a sign that the ploy pretending that she enjoyed meeting with him was already paying off. Now if the plan of getting her out of the country would work as quickly—but so far, no luck. Saturday morning found her sitting on the porch swing, waiting for the Commandant to pick her up as promised. At ten o'clock sharp, driving himself, he pulled up along the low stone wall in front of the farmhouse and peeped the horn. Nettie got into the car and sank into the luxurious leather seats. "I don't know much about automobiles, what kind is this?" she inquired.

"It's a Rolls-Royce. I'm sure it has some particular name or number, but I have to admit I don't know that much about automobiles either," he laughed.

He had such an easy laugh that it put her somewhat at ease. He drove right up on the main road, which told her that it hadn't been mined, yet, anyway. He stopped at a checkpoint and went into a small building just off the road. The soldiers at the checkpoint were not shy at staring at the young woman and Nettie wondered what they were thinking and decided she was glad she didn't know the answer to that. It was a relief when the Commandant returned and they resumed on their way, away from those prying eyes. They bumped over a rough dirt road that ran parallel to the beach. When they came to a deep ravine, he stopped and announced that they would walk from here. He retrieved a picnic basket from the back seat and she followed him down into the ravine and back up the other side. A few hundred feet further he put the basket down on a large boulder that sat on the edge of the cliff and stated that this looked like a good place to stop. Nettie agreed and took a seat on the boulder while the Commandant unfolded a blanket he had also brought and laid it on a nearby mound of earth a few yards away.

As before, Nettie opened her book and began to read where they had left off. After a few minutes she looked up to find him looking out over the channel. She stopped and it was a moment before he realized that she was no longer reading.

She gently asked, "Do you not like 'Treasure Island'?"

"Yes, it's a lot of fun. I was thinking that this was a perfect place to read the story." He then changed the subject as he asked, "Did you come here often? I mean you don't live that far away."

Nettie hesitated, she didn't really want to reveal much of herself to this man, but she had to say something. "I came here quite often. As a young child, my father would bring my brother Guillaume and me to the beach and we would walk along the shore and the cliffs. We would find shells and all kinds of things that would wash up on shore. After the war he wasn't strong enough to walk very far so I would come with my friends and spend summer afternoons playing and having cookouts. I haven't come here often since I left college."

"Why is that?"

She shrugged, "I was busy with work and helping with the farm, especially after my father died. It was just never the same." Without waiting for a reply she picked up the book again and started reading where she had left off.

The following Monday Clea popped her head into Nettie's classroom and motioned for her to come out into the hall. "I just received some new nail polish, do you want to come over after school and try some?" she asked.

"Sure, I'm not doing anything. I'll meet you downstairs after school."

After the last bell rang, they met on the front steps and walked to the Farve house a few blocks away.

They made themselves comfortable in the living room and they set about clipping and filing their nails while discussing the usual topic, the war. Nettie glanced out the front picture window and indicated with her head the house across the street and teased, "So, does Rolfe stop by for a cup of sugar once in awhile?"

Clea smirked, "No, he doesn't stop by for sugar or *anything else* either."

They both laughed.

After a few minutes Clea sobered and asked, "So, Nett, how many soldiers did you see when you went to the beach?"

"Hmmm," Nettie replied as she tried to shape one of her nails "I don't know."

"Well, how many do you *think?*"

"Oh, dozens I guess."

"Did they have mines in the water?"

"I guess."

"What kinds of mines?"

Exasperated, Nettie put down her file and stated, "How the hell should I know?"

Clea merely raised her eyes and examined her while she kept on filing a nail. "Oh," was all Nettie could say when the sudden realization hit her. "I'll pay more attention next time," she promised as she lowered her eyes and went back to work on her nails.

Chapter 14

That Wednesday was the third meeting of Nettie's and Rolfe's book club and they met again in his office after school was dismissed.

After Nettie tired of reading and closed the book, Rolfe inquired, "Did you know that I was invited to the Feast of All Saints at the convent?"

"How nice," commented Nettie. "They have a nice dinner every year and most of the town comes."

"Did they invite the previous Commandant?"

"No. He wasn't very popular," admitted Nettie cautiously.

"Then I feel privileged."

"You should," she stated simply.

At that moment there was a commotion outside in the hallway. Startled, Nettie jumped up from the rocking chair. Rolfe jumped up and went around the desk and flung open the top drawer and pulled out a revolver. He hurried to the door, but before opening it, he turned toward Nettie and told her to get behind the desk. She sprinted around to the other side of the massive wooden structure and crouched down.

Seeing that she was out of sight, Rolfe flung opened the door and the raised voices came to a sudden halt. "What is going on?" he demanded.

Nettie could make out Frederick's voice as the boy explained, "Excuse me, Herr Commandant, but these two ladies insist that they talk to you personally and would not explain what it was in regards to."

"If we could just talk to you, Herr Commandant. In private."

Recognizing the voice, Nettie stood up and advanced around the desk. "Aunt Elita?"

"Nettie! What…"

"You know this woman?" quizzed Rolfe.

"Of course, she is my mother's sister, and" pointing to the second woman standing next to her aunt, "that is Madam Mailliez, Adele's and Anna's mother."

"Then do come in," he offered as he set the revolver down on the desk. "Nettie, I shall see you Saturday."

Nettie took her cue and gathered up her belongings and left the room. What could that be about she wondered as she walked down the stairs and walked to the library to retrieve her bicycle.

It was not until the next morning that her question was answered. As she stood on the steps of the school, her colleagues filled her in on the details.

"Aimee and Adele were called up for service. They are to leave next Monday," informed Margarethe.

"They are children!" fumed Francois. "What was the government thinking when it went along with this?" They all knew he was referring to the Compulsory Labor Force that the Germans, with approval from the French government, had initiated just that spring. The few that had been selected from Blanc Fleur had either gone voluntarily months ago or had run off to join the Resistance.

"Adele is just seventeen and Aimee is still sixteen," sniffled a red-eyed Anna. "Are they that desperate that they are stealing France's children?"

"What did Aunt Elita and your mother talk to Rolfe about?" asked Nettie.

"They begged him to help," stated Anna simply.

"And will he?"

"He said that he would see what he could do. It appears their names were on a list that Commandant Neumann submitted a year ago."

Francois rolled his eyes. "I'll believe it when I see it."

The last bell rang just then and they went in their separate directions.

As it turned out Francois did not have long to wait to find out that he was wrong. The next afternoon as they were finishing their lunches on the school steps, Adele and Aimee came running out of Headquarters. They were jumping up and down and hanging onto each other and squealing in excitement. They skidded to a stop before the group of befuddled teachers.

"Guess what?" they screeched in unison.

"Adele tell me right now!" ordered her older sister.

"You're no fun!" she stated before answering. "The Commandant couldn't do anything about getting us off the list for compulsory service, *but*, we are to be stationed here."

"We are going to work for him," added Aimee. "Isn't that great? *And he is going to pay us!*"

The teachers were visibly relieved for the sake of the young women.

"Run home and tell everyone," ordered Anna.

"OK!" They answered in unison and both ran off, still jumping up and down.

"Before I just hated the man, now I feel sorry for him," commented Francois.

"Why?" laughed Clea.

"Well, not only does he have that bumble headed aide, he now has two teenage girls, *those* teenage girls, in his way. This may win us the war."

Nettie was in a good mood as she waited for Rolfe the next day. As before, he pulled up to the front of the house at 10 o'clock sharp. He spoke first after she got in. "Since we finished 'Treasure Island' on Wednesday, I was wondering what you selected for today." Nettie reached into her bag and pulled out two volumes and replied, "'Call of the Wild' by Jack London. See, I have one in French and one in German."

"Oh. What is it about?"

"It's about sled dogs in Alaska."

"Oh."

"Its really good," she rushed to assure him. "It has a lot of adventure in it."

"I'm sure it has."

"Don't you like dogs?"

"Of course I do. I have one at home. I just never associated them with great literature."

Nettie surprised even herself by laughing, "There is a first for everything."

When they reached the cliffs and Rolfe exited the automobile to check in at the small office, Nettie looked around and made mental notes of the number of people and equipment and the layout of the area. They went to the same area as before and Nettie took her place on the boulder. She read several chapters before she closed the book. "I'll stop here. I know I'm tired when I start reading in German and slip back into French."

"That's fine, I was following along in my book," he assured her.

Perhaps because she was feeling so comfortable with him, she asked, "You know a lot about my family. Tell me about yours, Rolfe."

"Well, I was born and raised in Wurttemberg. I was still at University when I married my childhood sweetheart, Gretchen. We have three children: Maria is the oldest, she is ten, Wilhelm who is eight, and Elisabeth who just turned seven. My family moved in with my parents a couple of years ago. My wife works as a bookkeeper at the same place I used to…before the war."

"Do they enjoy living with your parents?"

He shrugged and absently fanned the pages of the book he stilled held. "My parents have been a help looking after the children while

Gretchen works, plus it has saved us a lot of money. Of course, I wish…"

"That you were there?"

He nodded slowly. Nettie felt uncomfortable and sought to change the topic.

"Were you always a soldier?"

"Yes and no. I went into the military after school and served several years before I left to study at university. In 1939 I volunteered before I was drafted and was able to chose whom I served under."

"You wanted to serve under Rommel?"

"Yes. His father was a school teacher as is my father. They have been friends of my family for years. I figured if I had to serve then I couldn't select a better person or soldier." He thought for a moment before throwing his head back and laughing out loud.

Nettie looked at him curiously and said, "What is it?"

He stopped laughing and replied, "I was just thinking of the time I was with Rommel's entourage. It was during a battle and we came across a field hospital. Well, Rommel said to his driver that he should stop in for a moment and pay our respects to the patients and the hospital staff." Here he stopped, obviously trying not to laugh out loud again.

"What is so funny about that?" a puzzled Nettie asked.

"Well, most of us went inside the hospital and Herr Rommel inquired about the welfare of the patients and the supply of medicine." Here he stopped to catch his breath before he continued. "And somewhere along the tour he realized that not only were the patients British, the staff was too!"

"It was…"

"Yes. The Great Rommel had accidentally visited a British field hospital!" At that Nettie laughed in merriment at the story. "Are you teasing me?"

"No. It really did happen."

"What did he do then?"

"We all retreated out of the hospital and drove away. Quickly, I may add!" He laughed again.

After a moment of silence, she asked gently, "Did you see much action in North Africa?"

"After becoming part of the Afrika Korps, my first action was during the Siege of Tobruk which began in April of 1941 and went on for months. Then it was the Battle of Gazala, Battle of El Alamein, the Battle of the Kasserine Pass. We went back and forth between Tunsia, Lybia, and Eygpt for over two years."

"Must have been…difficult."

"It was. But at least you knew who the enemy was. The civilians were clustered in the cities and they were out of the way." Clearly uncomfortable with this topic, he stood up and reached for the picnic basket and blanket set nearby. He spread the blanket on the ground between them and sat down. Nettie slid off the boulder and joined him as he pulled out the food he had brought. She looked on in amazement as he pulled out oranges and sardines, items she hadn't seen in years.

As she began to fill her plate, he asked, "So, tell me a story."

Her hand stopped in midair as it reached toward a large, juicy orange. "What?"

"Tell me a story. Like what was the most memorable day of your life?" Seeing her unhappy expression he hastily added, "What is the happiest and or memorable day of your life?"

Nettie picked up the orange and sat back on her heels, feeling somewhat relieved. She then snapped her fingers and cocked her head as she came up with, "Well, when I was living in Paris I saw Charles Lindbergh after he made his transatlantic flight."

"Really?"

"It was the end of May in 1927 and I was just finishing up my first year of classes. I was in my dorm room when I heard my friend Louis calling to me from the alley. I asked him what he wanted and he said that Lindbergh's plane had just been spotted off the Irish coast and it looked like he was going to make it to Paris. A bunch of us got together and went out to Le Bourget Airport and waited. It was after dark before we could hear the engine of his plane. And the crush of people! It was a wonder that he didn't land on the crowd! And after he landed he was nearly trampled by everyone coming at him!" She stopped at this point and looked at Rolfe and feeling rather awkward finished, "I guess it's rather silly."

"Why? I would have liked to have been there to see history being made. *Good* history I should add. If you understand what I mean?"

Nettie, understanding, nodded.

Rolfe filled his plate and went to sit down on the boulder, while Nettie remained seated on the blanket, facing him. As they began eating, he looked out over the channel and motioned toward the water. "You know that the invasion will be here. On these beaches."

Nettie was caught off guard at this remark. "Do you really think so?"

He nodded. "They say it will be at Calais, but it won't. It will be here. Just a matter of time."

Nettie made her face expressionless. She didn't want to look too hopeful, at least not in front of him. As the silence became uncomfortable, she cocked her head and asked, "You said you went to university. What did you study?"

"I studied accounting and then I went to work for my uncle's factory."

"Oh. What did he make at his factory?" she politely inquired.

"Pickles. It was a pickling factory."

"They didn't...ah...make..."

"Yes. They made *sour kraut* there. That *is* what you were going to ask, isn't it?"

She had to admit it was.

He reached down and picked up three apples. Standing up, he threw two of them into the air and proceeded to juggle them. Nettie was surprised to find that he was quite accomplished and laughed. "Why Rolfe, I never knew you were so talented."

He glanced at her out of the corner of his eye and replied, "You have no idea of the juggling act I do."

Chapter 15

Much to Nettie's consternation, she was enjoying the trips to the cliffs and the chats in his office more and more. The weather was holding in to October and they were able to continue going there on Saturdays. Her friends would ask about her outings with the Commandant and she would tell them what they were reading. On Mondays she had a standing invitation to work on her nails and relay what she could remember from her trip to the beach. The conversations that she had with Rolfe were kept to herself. She wasn't sure why. She hadn't even told them about his real job, that as an accountant at a pickle factory. Perhaps they wouldn't be as amused as she had been, or they would be bored with such stories.

But mostly she felt ashamed for enjoying her time with him. It had been so long since she had discussed literature with an adult. Her mother and Nana didn't have time to read and her colleagues were busy with their own lives and problems brought on by the war. After finishing "Call of the Wild," they had read "Tom Sawyer". While Rolfe had enjoyed reading the American novel, he asked that they read something of more substance and preferably French. After giving him several options he settled on "Les Miserables" by the revered French author, Victor Hugo.

On November 1st, All Saints Day, the convent opened its doors to approximately one hundred of the town's inhabitants. The twenty or so nuns in residence would clear the first floor of the convent of furniture and set up tables and chairs for the guests. It came as no surprise to anyone, especially Nettie, that Rolfe was seated next to her at the same table. The seating arrangements were far from luxurious, as they consisted of a door supported by two sawhorses and the bench on which they sat was hard and backless.

"Do the Sisters do this once a year?" inquired Rolfe.

"No, they actually do this three times a year. Besides All Saints Day, they hold this at Easter and again on May 30th, which is St. Joan's Feast Day. She is, of course, the Patroness of France. They invite different people to each feast and between the three feasts, they are able to invite all those who would like to participate."

"Then I feel honored to be the only German invited."

"You're not. They invite Frederick to the Easter celebration."

"This town seems unusually fond of my young aide."

"Oh we are." Spoke up Sister Stephan from across the makeshift table. "I couldn't help but overhear what you were talking about. He has always been the friendliest and most helpful of young men. If we Sisters ever need anything, we just call on him. He is so handy with a hammer and nails."

"Really?" asked a puzzled Rolfe.

"Oh yes," she went on, "and he even installed a bathtub upstairs. Wasn't that nice?"

"He must be a very popular member of the parish."

"Oh, he's not Catholic," she said with a wave of her hand. A few seconds later she must have realized that she had babbled too much as she quickly excused herself, stating that she must help with the serving.

It was late afternoon before the Dupres set out for their farm. The fellowship had been most welcomed and pleasant. Even her mother and Nana had commented that they must try to get into town more often and visit.

As they reached the driveway to the farmhouse, her mother turned to Nettie and said, "Nett, would you go to the distillery and fetch me another box of canning jars? I think I'll make another batch of apple butter."

"Sure," she replied to her mother's request, and set off down the path to the distillery. As she neared the building, she noticed that the door was not only shut as usual, but latched as well. She had just been in there that morning, packing away bushel baskets that people had borrowed during the harvest and had just now returned. She remembered just shutting the door thinking that she would return with another load, but she had gotten busy in the house and didn't get a chance before they had headed to town.

The hair on her neck stood up as she advanced toward the door and unlatched the double doors. Pulling one of the doors open she looked in. Nothing seemed amiss at first glance, but then she glanced down and she gasped as she saw footprints all around her. It had rained the night before and the areas not covered with grass had been slightly muddy. Her footprints from that morning had been obliterated, so whomever they belonged to had come after her visit that morning. The footprints continued inside and pieces of still-damp mud were scattered everywhere. But after closer examination, Nettie could tell that they had only been interested in the empty oak barrels that were stacked everywhere. "Must have been soldiers looking for brandy," she thought to herself. Of course there were none to be found. Then a horrible thought came to her as she grabbed the ladder leaning next to the wall and placed it against the wide shelves holding the barrels. She scaled the ladder in seconds, only to find that what she had feared was true. The two barrels holding the electronic equipment were gone. Fear gripped her as she stared at the empty spaces in the top corner of the top shelf. But then she looked around her. Nothing was disturbed. The Germans would have simply smashed all of the barrels in their search. Whom ever had done this had put everything back in its place. She climbed down the ladder and went back outside and took another look at the prints. One set was small and narrow, obviously from a woman. Work boots, not the type of boots that were worn by the German soldiers, made the other two sets. She followed the prints to the clearing and on a hunch that proved to be correct, found them again on the back road where they ended next to the tracks of a dray and a team of horses. She doubted even more that the Germans would use horses; only the natives would do that. She sighed as she walked back to the distillery for the canning jars. She wondered why they hadn't just asked her for the equipment, but she had to admit she was somewhat relieved to have them off the Dupre property.

Later, before going to the house, Nettie went to the work shed and found the door still locked and no telltale footprints. Either they hadn't known of the supplies in the workshed or were not interested in radio parts.

When she told her mother and Nana, they were very concerned.

"Perhaps you should destroy the remaining supplies in the shed," suggested her mother, "in case they come back."

"If they didn't find them the first time, I doubt they would come back. I'm sure they think they got everything."

Nana looked thoughtful and wondered out loud, "You know, very few people even knew about the equipment. I wonder if Pierre or Terese might be involved somehow?"

"Well I wish they had said something to *us*. I mean we are their family."

"True, Nett. But perhaps it is better that they didn't," reasoned Nana.

"Perhaps," Nettie replied, but still felt a mixture of anger and resentment.

The following Saturday dawned chilly and overcast, typical for Normandy in November. Rolfe picked Nettie up and they drove to the cliffs. They made their way past the guards who now merely waved them on after a brief chat with Rolfe. They walked to their usual spot above the cliffs, overlooking the beach. Nettie took her seat on the boulder and wrapped a blanket around herself to keep out the brisk wind. Rolfe took his seat opposite her on the mound of earth. He buttoned his coat to his chin and laughed, "I guess this will be the last time we can come here…this season anyway." He took out his German translation of "Les Miserable" and opened to the chapter that they had left off on the previous Wednesday.

With Nettie following along in her French copy, Rolfe cleared his throat and began Reading, "'Book Fourth, Javert Derailed. He walked with drooping head for the first time in his life, and likewise, for the first time in his life, with his hands behind his back…'" Nettie looked over at Rolfe. She wondered if he was sorry to read such a massive piece of work, but he had been so keen on reading this novel that she had decided not to try and talk him out of it. "'For several hours, Javert had ceased to be simple. He was troubled; that brain, so limpid in its blindness, had lost its transparency; that crystal was clouded. Javert felt duty divided within his conscience, and he could not conceal the fact from himself.'"

"Would you like to read?" Rolfe asked as he interrupted himself.

"No, do go on," Nettie insisted as she raised the book back up before her face.

He continued on…"'One thing had amazed him,—this was that Jean Valjean should have done him a favor, and one thing petrified him,—that he, Javert, should have done Javert a favor…'"

Nettie listened as he read the familiar story of the policeman, Javert, as he struggled to come to terms with his conscious in letting the prisoner, Jean Valjean, go free.

"'...society is not perfect, authority is complicated with vacillation, a crack is possible in the immutable, judges are but men, the laws may err, tribunals may make a mistake! To behold a rift in the immense blue pane of the firmament!'" At this point Rolfe stopped.

Nettie peeped around the side of her book. "Are you all right?" She noticed his face had begun to look weary.

"I am just tired of reading. Can you finish this chapter?" he asked.

She nodded and read to the end of the chapter, finishing with the last sentences, "'Javert remained motionless for several minutes gazing at this opening of shadow; he considered the invisible with a fixity that resembled attention. The water roared. All at once he took off his hat and placed it on the edge of the quay. A moment later, a tall black figure, which a belated passer-by in the distance might have taken for a phantom, appeared erect upon the parapet of the quay, bent over towards the Seine, then drew itself up again, and fell straight down into the shadows; a dull splash followed; and the shadow alone was the secret of the convulsions of that obscure form which had disappeared beneath the water.'"

"He killed himself?" asked an incredulous Rolfe. "Just jumped off a bridge because he let Jean Valjean go?"

"Its not that easy," Nettie responded. She drew the blanket tighter around her as the winds had begun to pick up. "Remember when we did the characterizations for Fantine and the Bishop? Perhaps we can start on Valjean and Javert."

Rolfe nodded and Nettie continued. "Valjean demonstrates the struggle of good and evil in men. He is corruptible." She searched for her words. How had she described Valjean to her students so many years ago? A lifetime ago? "It says that man is perfectible, can become a better person by their actions, by forgiving himself or herself along with forgiveness by God…"

"Have you forgiven yourself?" he asked with an unexpected suddenness that caught Nettie off guard for a heartbeat.

"I haven't done anything that has required me to forgive myself or that required God's forgiveness," she responded firmly.

"It must be so nice to be so perfect," he answered, his gray eyes trained on her face. She felt a flush rushing to her face and shot back, "And Javert is the opposite. He is incorruptible and obedient to the law. He enforces the law and makes society live by the laws he believes in. When he finds that the law is fallible he can't stand to reject the values he has held all his life and he chooses to kill himself rather than changing." She caught her breath and continued, "Are you like Javert? Can you not let anyone deviate from your laws?" His look stopped her from continuing.

In a cold voice that was new to Nettie he stated, "Mademoiselle, I am paid to enforce the laws of the Third Reich, and I intend to do just that. I am not paid to forgive others who are running their own agenda. I will seek them out and destroy them." With that he lunged forward in order to stand up. Startled, Nettie jumped up and found herself standing on the rock, looking down at an angry Rolfe.

He picked up the uneaten lunch, threw the book inside the basket and whipped the blanket over his arm. With his free hand he reached up and grabbed Nettie's arm and jerked her to the ground with the words, "It's getting cold and it's time to go." With that announcement he started off down the trail to the car, leaving Nettie to hurry behind him. At one point the path narrowed and took them dangerously close the edge of the cliff. Nettie's eyes drilled into the Commandant's back. She began to think that if she just reached out and gave a firm shove, he would lose his balance and fall over the cliff, onto the rocks below. She knew the guards were too far away and couldn't see this part of the terrain. She wondered briefly if the Third Reich would believe her unfortunate luck with German Commandants. Yes, it was tragic the way they seemed to have accidents in her company! She raised her hand up, aimed for the middle of his back. She hesitated; she wanted to hate this man, to be rid of him. Well, didn't she? Her hand was still raised when he abruptly turned around and grabbed her hand and placed her arm under his.

"The path is rather dangerous here, we wouldn't want any accidents, would we?" He planted a big smile on his face as he continued marching back to the car. Nettie lowered her eyes only to notice the shadows that their forms cast on the ground.

"That's just what I was thinking," she answered.

Later, in the car, Nettie stared out the window. She was frightened. Frightened because the conversation between them had ceased, frightened because she had come so close to pushing him off the cliff without a second thought. Oddly, she was frightened because that was all she would have felt for murdering him, not guilt and certainly not remorse. Perhaps the latter concerned her the most. But what had stopped her from doing it? Maybe her conscience was still lurking in her soul after all.

Desperate to break the uneasy silence, Nettie spoke up. "I won't be able to meet with you for several weeks. We, the teachers, are going to start planning the Christmas pageant soon and I will be busy until after the holidays."

He nodded and after a moment replied, "That would be a great activity for my men and the townspeople to do together, don't you think?"

The faces of her colleagues and students flashed before her eyes. "Ahhhh…yes. It could be something we do together. I'll ask the others at the first meeting, OK?"

"Great," he smiled. "Here we are." He turned the car into the Dupre driveway. Nettie was never so relieved to get away as she pushed the door open and jumped out, slamming the door behind her. He waved as he backed the car out and drove toward town. Nettie watched him disappear into the distance. Yes, she could hardly wait to tell the others all right.

Chapter 16

As expected, the news of the offered help did not go over well with Nettie's friends at school.

"I can't believe you said it was OK," moaned Margarethe. "Like we don't see enough of the krauts NOW."

"*What* could I say? Besides, this way we control what they do," explained Nettie, hoping she sounded convincing. She noticed Clea staring off into space with a thoughtful look on her face.

"I think it's a good idea," said the pretty blonde. After noticing all the looks aimed at her she added, "Hey, I've heard the church choir and it could use all the help it can get."

"I don't want any of those krauts in my choir," sniffed Francois.

"I am sure they can get enough for their own choir," assured Nettie. "I am sure they will do anything we ask."

"Maybe they could be the asses in the Nativity Play," snipped Francois. The others broke into laughter except Marie-Claire who tried to look disapprovingly at the group. Nettie put her head in her hands. What was she getting herself and all of them into, anyway?

"OK, OK. We will make the best of it. Let's start on the basic set up for the pageant," interjected Mr. LaPierre, trying to bring the group to order. "First of all, let's try to keep the running time to an hour and a half. Do you all agree?"

"Lets make it closer to two hours," suggested Clea.

"Well, OK," agreed Mr. LaPierre. "I guess that would give us time to do all that we would like and we do need extra time for the Germans."

They got down to business and decided who would be on what committee and what would be presented in the pageant. Preliminary rehearsals would start the following Sunday afternoon.

The following weeks went by quickly. School ended for the winter months and everyone was either busy with the Nativity play or in one of the choirs. Nettie was appointed to the job of designing and building the set for the Nativity play. She had pretended to be hurt that she was not assigned to one of the choirs, but the others felt they were to suffer enough with the Germans being included. The first order of business was to secure the help of several soldiers to help in the physical building of the set. This she quickly accomplished, and among them was Frederick.

Following her simple design, the Germans went to work under Nettie's supervision. She was pleased to find that they worked hard, the pounding and sawing only interrupted by the oaths aimed at Frederick, who was constantly tripping over boards or dropping hammers and nails.

"Du schize kopf, watch what you are doing!" was a common phrase to be heard, usually followed by an ear cuff. Frederick would simply respond by rubbing his ear and walking away, which seemed to infuriate the other soldiers even more. Often Frederick would stay and continue to work after the other men had left, his long, graceful fingers holding a nail while he pounded it in with his other hand. His long legs stepped over the debris that littered the ground. The Germans thought of him as a klutz, but Nettie knew differently. She also knew better than to ask why he invited such abuse on himself. It was during one of his solitary work times that Nettie asked him, "Will you be at the pageant, Frederick?"

"No, my people don't celebrate...celebrate like this."

As his back was turned he didn't see Nettie's eyebrows furrow in puzzlement. His "people" seemed to enjoy celebrating more than "her people."

Frederick turned back around. "Did we decide if the sheep were going on the left or the right side of the stable?"

"Oh, ahhh...hmmm. I don't remember," Nettie admitted. "I'll go get the plans we drew up and double check. I'll be back in a minute." She made her way from the staging area in the courtyard where the pageant was to take place and through a side gate that led down an alley to the convent. The headquarters for the pageant had been ensconced in the basement of the ancient building. She let herself in the unlocked side door and hurried down the dark stairwell. She found no one else around, but was not concerned because she knew where the plans were kept. At the bottom of the dark stairwell, she reached up and pulled on a string that turned on a light that illuminated a few feet into the darkness.

She could make out the tables on the other side of the room and turned on the light over the table that held her stable plans. Finding what she needed she rolled the paper up and tucked it under her arm. Just as she reached up to pull the string and turn it off, her attention was captured by something sparkling about twenty feet away. Several racks of costumes lined the wall. Keeping the light on she walked over to the closest rack and realized the costume that caught her eye must belong to one of the three wise men. She pulled out the costume and saw that it was of Arabian design. She knew that would be Balthasar and Mr. LaPierre would be playing that role. She replaced the costume and pulled out the one next to it. The costume was of Indian design and Nettie knew that would be Anna's Gaspar costume. "That would leave Melchior," she said to herself as she pulled out the Asian style costume to examine. She was surprised to find that it was heavier than the other two. She put it back on the rack and looked at it much more closely.

Surely they could not expect Clea to comfortably wear this bulky, heavy costume. She lifted one of the long, wide sleeves and something didn't seem quite right. She put her hand in and turned it inside out. It took her a moment to realize what was different about this costume, or should she say, costumes. One was tucked carefully inside the other. Why would they need two identical Melchior costumes? She carefully rearranged the two costumes to how they looked when she found them. An idea crossed her mind as she picked up the roll of paper she had placed on the floor and turned off the burning lights and hurried up the stairs to the fresh air.

She made her way back to the staging area and found Frederick lounging on a pile of hay. He was singing an unfamiliar song in English and Nettie had to concentrate to understand the words.

"I don't know that song, Frederick. Could you repeat the words?"

"Sure," he replied, and proceeded to repeat the following poem:
I heard the bells on Christmas day
Their old familiar carols play
And mild and sweet the words repeat
Of peace on earth, good will to men

I thought how as the day has come,
The belfries of all Christendom
Had roll'd along the unbroken song
Of peace on earth, good will to men

And in despair I bow'd my head:
"There is no peace on earth," I said,
"For hate is strong, and mocks the song
Of peace on earth, good will to men."

Then pealed the bells more loud and deep:
"God is not dead, nor doth He sleep;

The wrong shall fail, the right prevail,
With peace on earth, good will to men."

"Who wrote that?"

"An American by the name of Longfellow. He is referring to the American Civil War in the poem, but it does fit during these times, doesn't it?"

Nettie nodded sadly. "All too well." Changing the topic she finished, "Here are the plans. The sheep go on the left side of the stable. I'm tired, I think I'll go home." She handed him the plans and turned around and hurried away.

"Good-bye, Nett. I'll see you tomorrow," he called after her.

She didn't answer. She wanted to get away. For some reason the poem had depressed her. Would right prevail? She wondered.

The mystery of the costumes stayed in the back of Nettie's mind as busy days flew by. Three days before the pageant and four before Christmas, Frederick, in his dress uniform, knocked on the Dupre door. He carried an engraved invitation for 'Fraulien Bernadette Dupre' to a Christmas party that was to be given by Rolfe. Nettie invited him in to wait while she went into the kitchen to discuss the invitation with her mother.

"Christmas Eve? There is so much going on that night," exclaimed her mother. "Are you sure you want to go?"

"The play will be over by 7:30 and we have several hours before Midnight Mass. I am sure I can fit a party in there. Besides, what reason could I give for not going?"

Her mother shrugged. "I guess you are going then."

"Don't worry, I'm sure everyone else is going. And I am sure I can spend the night at the convent." Nettie returned to the entryway where Frederick remained obediently standing. She smiled at the young man. "Please tell the Commandant that I will be attending his party."

Something flashed in his eyes but he remained silent and bowed in reply. He straightened up and said, "Forgive me, but I need to retrieve a package from the car." With that he walked out the door and returned with a small box that he handed to Nettie. "This is a gift from the Commandant." She took the box from him and opened the lid. Inside were several glass tree ornaments. As she lifted one shaped like a fruit basket out of the box, Frederick spoke up, "It's an old German tradition to have these ornaments on the Christmas tree. Each of them represents something. The fruit basket represents generosity." He then pointed to each of the others in turn and explained, "The flower basket is for good wishes, the angel is for God's guidance, the pine cone is for fruitfulness, the bird is for joy, the fish is for Christ's blessing, the rabbit is for hope, the teapot is for hospitality, the rose is for affection, the heart for true love, the Santa for goodwill, and…" he reached into the box and pulled out a little glass house. It was milky white with a red door and blue shutters, topped off with a brown roof. He gently waved the tiny white house that was hung on a thin, red ribbon in her face and added, "Last but not least, the house, which stands for protection."

"Oh," she said in surprise at receiving a gift from Rolfe. "I will thank him personally when I see him."

"Of course." With that he turned and left the house and walked to the car parked in the road and drove off. Nettie watched as the car got smaller and smaller in the distance before shutting the door and walking into the kitchen to show her mother the gift from Rolfe.

After Nettie explained the meaning of each of the ornaments, her mother commented, "It's too bad we never picked up on the tradition of having a Christmas tree. But I guess you can place them among the greens over the fireplace." Agreeing, Nettie took them to the next room and carefully tied each of the tiny ornaments to the fragrant evergreen branches that lined the mantle.

Later, as the three of them were sitting down to dinner in the kitchen, the sound of breaking glass was heard from the next room. Nettie rushed into the living room and found that one of the small ornaments had fallen from the mantle and smashed into hundreds of tiny pieces on the hardwood floor. As she bent over to pick up the bigger pieces her mother appeared behind her and said, "Oh dear, that's too bad. Which one was it?"

"The rabbit."

"What did the rabbit signify again?"

"Hope."

* * *

As it turned out, not everyone was going to the Commandant's party. Of the town's natives, only Mr. LaPierre, Anna and Adele had received invitations. Clea was not invited, but that hardly surprised anyone. Aimee, as one of his new employees, had been rather put out; but, as her own mother pointed out, she was too young.

Thursday, the day before Christmas Eve, Nettie packed a small overnight bag and walked into town. She and several other women who were involved with the pageant and lived out of town had taken the Sisters up on the invitation to spend the night in the convent. After a long day of final preparations, they all gathered in the common room of the convent and passed around plates of cookies, candies, and other sweets, all washed down with glasses of cider.

They sang Christmas carols and discussed the war in the safety of the convent. A few asked Nettie questions about the Commandant, but Nettie, feeling uncomfortable, would only supply a brief answer.

Later, as Nettie and Marie-Claire sat on their beds in Marie-Claire's small bedroom, they reminisced about the past and when Marie-Claire started to talk about the future of the school and what she would like to see happen with the school after the war, she noticed Nettie had become silent.

"What's the matter, Nett?"

Her friend didn't reply for several moments, but then said, "Oh Marie, I don't try to think of the future. I…don't know if I will have one."

"Nettie! How can you say that? You must have hope that all this will end. Soon."

Nettie gave a half smile. "My hope seems to have shattered. Just like that rabbit."

Marie-Claire gave her a puzzled look and Nettie explained about the ornament that had fallen from the mantle and broken.

"It's just an ornament, Nett. Nothing more and nothing less."

"Of course," Nettie replied, and she did want to believe that.

The next day was spent on the last-minute details and each saying under their breaths that this was the last time that Blanc Fleur was going to put on this extravagant pageant. All through the day Nettie noticed that Clea and Adele seemed to be having several whispered conversations that would end abruptly when anyone approached. She shrugged it off, telling herself that she was just getting too paranoid.

She and Frederick went to several farms and picked up the selected animals to be part of the scenery in the Nativity play. They double-checked the fences to ensure that the animals would not get loose.

As show time approached, Nettie changed into black workpants and a heavy black coat to keep out the winter chill. She would sit behind the stable and make sure everything held together and capture any escaping animals there may be. She found a small stool and placed it behind the back wall. She had already drilled a peep hole that she could look through and see nearly all of the stage. Her work completed, she took her seat and looked through the hole. The audience was already floating in and finding their choice seats. Rolfe had already found his place in the front row, surrounded by several men and women she did not recognize.

As darkness softly fell, the orchestra, such as it was, began to play a melody of traditional Christmas carols. The children's choir followed, and to Nettie's and everyone else's delight, they remembered all the words to the two songs they had been rehearsing for the last four weeks. The highlight and the centerpiece of the evening, the Nativity play, was next. Nettie perched on the edge of the stool as she strained to see the children in the upper grades playing Mary and Joseph making their way down the aisle toward the stable. She was relieved to see the donkey plodding along quietly. It would not be a pleasant sight if the donkey threw the 'pregnant' Mary and headed for the exit like a donkey did a few years ago. The younger children remembered that one for months. Sure, they couldn't remember their times' tables but they could remember the spectacle of a young girl being pitched over the head of a donkey!

Several choirs sang while the older children acted out the Nativity play. Mary and Joseph arriving in Bethlehem, being turned away from the lodging houses, Mary giving birth in a stable, and the angels appearing to the shepherds in the fields.

Nettie's back was sore from leaning over to see the action on the other side of the stable wall. She turned around and leaned back against the stable wall. The night was beautiful, although cold. She looked up and could make out the stars twinkling in the elements. A clear tenor began one of her favorite Christmas songs, "Holy Night." The words transported her back to a Christmas long before. Pierre and Terese were mere children. Nana played the piano while her mother sang that very song. Her father was there, pale and resting on the davenport. Odd, she had forgotten her mother sang so well and Nana played the piano. What had happened to the piano? It had disappeared from their home not long after that Christmas she was reliving. Then she remembered that it had been sold to pay for her father's funeral. A deep sadness engulfed her as she wished she were back at her living room with her family instead of sitting in the dark on a stool. She hadn't really thought about her brother and sister in weeks, but now found herself ready to give anything for another day with them, another Christmas with them. In her heart she felt instinctively that something was wrong with Pierre or

Terese or perhaps both of them. She wanted to talk to them one last time, but she knew that she had no idea of how to find them.

With the start of the song, "We Three Kings," she was jolted back to the present. Turning back around, she peeped through the hole to watch the "Royal Procession" wind its way toward the stable. All of the kings wore masks that were fashioned out of papier-mache'. Each of the masks and costumes reflected the part of the world from which each of the wise men had originated. First came Anna in the Turkish costume of Gaspar, the papier-mache mask portraying the face of a young European man. Next came Mr. LaPierre as Balthasar, the middle-aged Ethiopian wise man, followed by his entourage. Then Clea as Melchior, the venerable old wise man from Arabia and his following. Several small children, acting as attendants, carried banners, held a canopy over each king, and, of course, bearing gifts of gold, frankincense and myrrh. Nettie's attention was focused on Melchior. Something was not as it should be. The figure was tall and slender, the mask hiding any facial features. But after so many years of working and being friends with someone, Nettie realized it was not Clea in that costume. The kingly trio one by one paid homage to the Christ Child in the manger and then stood so that their backs were to the peep hole that Nettie had drilled and faced the audience. A long strand of hair had escaped the silk hood of the Melchior costume. Even in the dim light Nettie could easily see that it was too long and definitely not blonde in color. Gaspar's hand slowly reached out and without attracting any attention carefully tucked the stray lock back into the costume. Of course! It was Adele in that costume! But why?

At the end of the next song, the three Wise Men and their entourages made their way off the stage and down the side aisle. They walked to the end of the courtyard and then turned into the schoolhouse, at a side door leading down to the basement. Silently, in her dark clothing, Nettie slipped from around the stable and made her way up the side aisle and entered the schoolhouse via the front door. She walked as quickly as she could, not wanting to draw attention to herself as she rushed by children and adults getting ready to enter the courtyard for the multi-choir finale that was next on the agenda. The participants in the royal entourage were already coming up the back stairs when Nettie arrived. She stood there only a moment before Anna and Clea, their masks off, made their way up the stairs. The women saw her waiting for them and each of them grabbed an arm on each side and they walked down the hallway of the school.

"How did it go?" asked Clea, looking at Nettie out of the corner of her eye.

"I would say it went like clockwork," she answered. Clea and Anna smiled at each other and led Nettie to the front steps of the school where they watched the rest of the pageant.

At the end of the show, Nettie hooked up with her mother and Nana as they prepared to walk home with several neighbors from surrounding farms. Even though Rolfe had offered the services of his soldiers, they had decided to leave before Midnight Mass. Nettie realized it would be their first Christmas morning apart, but she would be home before noon, so it wouldn't be too unbearable. She walked them to the city gates before stopping and wishing all of them all a joyous Noel.

Anna and Adele, after seeing their families off, joined Nettie in the walk to the convent to get ready for the Commandant's party. She retrieved her dress from Marie-Claire's tiny wardrobe and held it up for inspection. It was poppy red and the color flattered Nettie's complexion and dark eyes. However, the style was at least eight years behind the times. The shoes that had been dyed to the same shade had also seen better days. "Oh well," she muttered to herself, knowing everyone else in town was in the same boat as she was. After she changed her underwear, she slipped the dress over her head and was dismayed at the reflection in the mirror that awaited her. Her face was drawn and looked more tired than she actually felt. Well, the face she knew she could fix with some cosmetics; however, there was nothing she could do about the dress that had one time clung to her curves but now simply hung on her thin frame. She unbraided her hair and brushed it out. It fell to the small of her back in waves. She fished out matching combs from her overnight bag and placed them in her hair as to keep the length out of her face. Marie-Claire came in as she finished dressing and complimented her on her outfit. As Nettie turned to go, Marie-Claire spoke. "You will be coming back tonight, won't you?"

"Oh, it will be too late to wal…Marie! What sort of question is that?" Nettie asked when she realized what her friend was actually asking.

"I wasn't born a nun. I know he looks at you."

Nettie looked her square in the eye. "Maybe you should start noticing how *I* look *at him*!" With that she opened the door and stomped out of the room, meeting Anna and Adele in the hall.

"What's wrong, Nett?" they asked.

"Nothing," she snapped as she led them down the stairs to a side door.

Marie-Claire watched from a window as her friends walked into the night. She said softly to herself, "No, you don't love him, but what you fear you find fascinating, and that, Nett, may be even worse."

The three women found the party at the Commandant's house in full swing. Alcohol flowed freely and sumptuous food was everywhere.

"Looks like the Germans are doing well," remarked Anna.

"I think tonight *I* will be doing well!" answered Adele as she headed for a platter holding a variety of cheese and breads.

"I take it Adele enjoys her job with Rolfe," commented Nettie.

"Oh yes. She says he is always slipping her and Aimee treats. And did you notice her coat? He gave her the coat for Christmas and gave Aimee one just like it in black."

"That was nice of him," observed Nettie.

"Maybe I should ask him for a job," whispered Anna.

"You do that," teased Nettie.

Just then Rolfe advanced toward them and started to introduce them around. The room was filled with a few of the locals, but most were officers stationed throughout the region. The women seemed to be a mix of German wives and French mistresses. At dinner they were seated at various tables scattered throughout the dining room and living room. Rolfe was seated at the head of the table where Nettie was seated. She sat on his right, with Adele to his left. Anna was seated on the other side of her sister. On the other side of Nettie was seated a Lieutenant Diehm with his date, an overly made-up French woman from Paris on the other side of him.

After village women who had been hired to cook and serve for this occasion placed beef, turkey and a vast assortment of vegetable dishes on the table, Rolfe stood up. "May I have your attention, please." Quickly the chatter ended and all eyes were focused on him. He raised his wine-filled glass and smiled. "First of all, I am happy to announce that my request for a leave has been approved and I leave for home on the 26th." With this bit of news an excited murmur raced through the room. He spoke again: "Since I will be with my family for New Years, I will take the opportunity to wish all of you a Frohe Weihnacten, a Joyeux Noel and a Happy New Year. May 1944 bring us happiness, new beginnings and joyous en…" Catching himself, he ended the sentence "peace."

"Here, here," seconded a voice from another table and all raised their glasses and took a drink. As Rolfe sat back down, Nettie leaned in his direction and commented, "It will be nice to visit your family again."

He nodded and replied softly, so only Nettie could hear, "It will be great to see them all again. Who knows when I will ever see them again…" A twinge of apprehension surged through Nettie as she looked into his face. She said nothing to him as the platters of food being passed around the table distracted her. In the back of her mind she wondered if he would try and avoid coming back to Blanc Fleur when his leave was up.

As she dug into the food in front of her, she caught the conversation between the French woman seated on the other side of Lieutenant Diehm and Anna and Adele. "My, look at you two." She smiled in a rather condescending way at Adele. "A couple of Normans I see." The sisters stopped eating and stared at her. "I mean that red hair! I can just see a bloodthirsty Viking when I look at you two! Of course those Bretons are worse, they're *really* English people you know!" she finished in a conspiratorial tone.

"And you…" She looked at Nettie, where are your people from?

"France, Madam," she answered quickly.

Rolfe broke in, "Her father is from Alsace…"

"Oh a German! And your mother is…?"

"A Moor, Madam," Nettie answered in a tone that indicated that the subject was closed.

The woman's smile faded. "Oh…"

"As I was saying Sophia, you will find them all *very French*, even if they are not from Paris." Sophia shrugged and turned to the officer sitting on the other side of her and ignored them, much to their relief.

After the meal was served by the caterers, Rolfe stood up and raised his glass and Announced, "I understand that this will not be news to those of you who aren't posted to out of the way places such as Blanc Fleur. But I just learned of this the other day and I am most excited by the news. My former superior officer, Erwin Rommel, has been appointed Commander of Northern France. It will be a pleasure to serve under him again." With that he raised his glass in salute. The other guests must have found this good news as it was greeted with a chorus of "That's wonderful" and "Here, here". Nettie and the sisters looked at each other across the table, unsure if they were to toast the good news of the enemy or not. They didn't.

The hour grew late and those wishing to attend Midnight Mass retrieved their coats and headed for the door. Most of the guests stayed behind to finish off the liquor and food. To Nettie's surprise, their host joined the group going to Mass.

"Aren't you leaving your own party?"

"I'll be back before they know I am gone," he stated with a dismissal wave of his hand. He stayed by her side until they were beside a storefront with a hidden doorway. He gently grasped her elbow and slowed her until everyone had passed them and then he moved her into the doorway, out of sight. She looked up at him in surprise.

"This is for you." He handed her a small doll in the shape of an elf. Attached to it was a small round container. "It's just candy. It is what we call a 'snow baby.'"

"Oh, it's cute. I also need to thank you for the ornaments that Frederick brought by the other day." She then became speechless that he had given her yet another gift. She looked up into his eyes as his hands went up to her face and he leaned forward. She shut her eyes to the inevitable. His soft lips brushed her forehead. Her eyes flew open as he said, "Merry Christmas, Nett. I want to thank you for all of your time and the joy of literature that you have shared with me."

"Even the dogs?" was all she could think to say, thankful the dark doorway hid her rosy cheeks.

"Even the dogs," he laughed. "Come, or we will never get a seat."

It was well after 2 a.m. when the three women made their way back to the convent with the Sisters who had also attended the service. After Nettie had turned off the lamp by the cot, Marie-Claire apologized to Nettie. "I am so sorry for what I said. I am sure you know what you are doing."

"Don't worry about it, Marie," she mumbled. As she laid there in the dark, she wondered if she really did know what she was doing. With her forearm she wiped at her forehead, trying to wipe off the lasting feel of his kiss.

Chapter 17

With the festivities of Christmas and the New Year over, life fell into a dull routine. With the weather cold and drab few felt like leaving their homes and venturing out. Rolfe returned to Blanc Fleur the 3rd of January. Many in the town were relieved to see him walking the streets again. Several, including Francois, kept whispering that "going on leave" might be euphemistic for his leaving permanently. Nettie was almost happy to devote two afternoons a week for reading with Rolfe. With school being closed for the season and little work to be done around the house and farm, the chance to go into town twice a week had become the highlight of her life. It was during this time right after his return that she noticed a slight change in his mood. He seemed slightly withdrawn, even detached from those around him. Nettie didn't dare ask him about his trip home, and he never offered any details other than it was great to see his family again and that he missed them. After engaging him in conversation concerning something they were reading, he would appear to return to his old self, but Nettie felt a change, although at first she shrugged it off to his sadness at leaving his family.

When he returned to Blanc Fleur, instead of meeting in his drafty office, they moved the literary discussions to his home. There they would relax in overstuffed chairs in front of a roaring fire and be waited on by his housekeeper, Madam Lamy. Occasionally Adele and Aimee would be summoned to help with the cooking or cleaning and Nettie would hear them laughing and talking in the other room. It was obvious that neither girl was overworked nor underfed; indeed, their families remarked that the girls were as fat and sassy now as they were before the war.

It was in this cozy setting that they spent many an hour pouring over the literature that Nettie provided. She was finding it harder and harder to locate items that were available in both German and French. She had already gone through what the library could provide and now was asking her friends and neighbors. Little by little, oblivious to Nettie, she was letting down her guard. After reading and discussing a chapter or section they fell into a comfortable routine of chatting about other things. At first they may talk about the weather, later farming and crops, and gradually they would talk about their families. He would talk about the letters from his wife and the welfare of his children and she would talk about her missing siblings. She was finding it easier to look into those gray eyes and feel comfortable there. She talked about living under German laws and the changes brought about by them. Things she couldn't always talk about with her friends—their problems always made hers look trivial, but she needed to voice them just the same and he seemed to listen. As before, she would tell others what book they were studying but never mention the conversations they had. She feared that it would be construed as a friendship with the man, when she was really just tolerating him. At least that is what she told herself.

She had come to enjoy discussing the classics with him, as he was bright and eager to learn. She was also finding him disconcertingly fascinating. Most people found him quite handsome; she had to admit that it was true. But it was more than just one trait that she found appealing. She would peer over her book while his head was bent over reading a passage from a page. She would study his dark blonde hair, cut into short, crisp waves that ended at the base of his skull in the back. The brows, the same shade of dark blonde hair, were narrow and long. The long lashes that framed the gray piercing eyes curled at the ends. She rather liked his chin, which was strong without being jutting. The chin compensated for the one feature of his that she didn't like, his lips. The lips were rather thin and drawn but she thought one tended to be drawn to his long, aquiline nose anyway. She would watch his long, tapered fingers turn the delicate pages of the books with ease. At the end of each meeting he would tell her how much he was learning from their time together. Always the gentleman, he would walk her to the town gates and say how much he was looking forward to their next session. Other than these sessions, she rarely saw him when she ran errands in town, or if she did it was by honest accident, or at least that is what she chose to believe.

It was the middle of February and Nettie arrived at Rolfe's house as usual. He let her in and as usual offered her some tea or coffee. As she settled into an overstuffed chair she noticed that when he settled down in the chair opposite her, he pulled a large piece of gray material onto his lap and reached toward a small sewing basket that was sitting on an end table next to the chair.

"What are you doing?" she asked.

He seemed surprised at the question and responded, "Oh, I ripped a seem on my uniform."

"Can't Madam Lamy or one of the girls do that?"

"Well Madam Lamy is off for a few days and the girls are helping Frederick catch up on some correspondence. So, what have you brought today?"

"I found a collection of plays by William Shakespeare. Are you familiar with his work?"

"Oh yes. I read Hamlet and Romeo and Juliet at University. Also, my accounting professor was a big fan. Every day he would write a quote from his plays or poems on the chalk board. I guess he wanted to break the monotony of an exciting topic such as accounting."

"Do you remember much about the plays and the quotes your instructor used?" Rolfe picked up a small sewing needle and neatly threaded it with a strand of gray thread.

"I vaguely remember the plays. I do remember some of the quotes. I guess I always enjoyed the quotes because they were timeless. They have as much meaning today as they did nearly four hundred years ago." He smiled and cocked his head and said,

"'Neither a borrower nor a lender be;
For loan oft loses both itself and friend,
And borrowing dulls the edge of husbandry.
This above all: to thine own self be true,
And it must follow, as the night day,
Thou canst not then be false to any man.'"
"Very good! That was from Hamlet."
"I also remember

"'What's in a name? That which we call a rose
By any other name would smell as sweet.'"
"That's from Romeo and Juliet. My favorite quote from that play goes like this:
"'When he shall die,
Take him out and cut him out in little stars,
And he will make the face of heaven so fine
That all the world will be in love with night,
And pay no worship to the garish sun.'"
"And of course there is 'A horse! A horse! My kingdom for a horse'!"
Nettie laughed and, thinking of another quote said:
"'Confess yourself to heaven;
Repent what's past; avoid what is to come.'"

Rolfe didn't answer. Instead he seemed to concentrate on the wad of material he was sewing. More to himself than to Nettie he said softly to himself:

"'I hold the world but as the world, Gratiano,
A stage, where every man must play a part,
And mine a sad one.

I am in blood
Stepp'd in so far that, should I wade no more,
Returning were as tedious as go o'er

O, my offence is rank, it smells to heaven;
It hath the primal eldest curse upon't,
A brother's murder.'"

He held up the dress uniform that he had been working on and quoted from Henry IV:
"'Company, villanous company, hath been the spoil of me.'"
Nettie starred at the dress coat. For some reason the swastikas with their black spinning legs captured her attention. Bottled up anger bubbled to the surface. She had meant to say it to herself, but instead came out of her mouth in a sharp tone:
"'My words fly up, thoughts remain below:
Words without thoughts never to heaven go.'"
He lowered the material to reveal his red, angry face and fiercely replied:

"'False face must hide what the false heart doth know.'"
Startled, Nettie stared at the angry face before her and replied with the first quote that her anxious mind could think of:
"'This was the most unkindest cut of all.'"

Gaining control over his emotions, Rolfe said:
"'Mend your speech a little,
Lest it may mar your fortunes.'"

Nettie, still in shock, got to her feet and looked at him.
"'The true beginning of our end.'"
Rolfe got to his feet and walked to the door and opened it with the words:
"'I do desire we may be better strangers.'"
Nettie grabbed her coat off the rack next to the door and exited without putting it on. She walked, oblivious to the cold, down the block and through an ally. Suddenly she realized that she was in back of the school and entered via the back door. She walked up the stairwell and entered her empty classroom. She sat at the teacher's desk and plopped the book of Shakespeare's plays that she had unconsciously clutched to herself since leaving the Commandant. It opened to the play Mcbeth. Nettie slipped her hand under the cover to shut the volume when her eyes went to the words on the page.
"'Macduff: Bleed, bleed, poor country!
Great Tyranny, lay thou thy basis sure,
For goodness dares not check thee: wear thou thy
Wrongs,
The title is affeered! Fare thee well, lord:
I would not be the villain that thou think'st
For the whole space that's in the tyrant's grasp
And the rich East to boot.

Malcolm: Be not offended:
I speak not as in absolute fear of you:
I think our country sink beneath the yoke,
It weeps, it bleeds, and each new day a gash
Is added to her wounds. I think withal

There would be hands uplifted in my right;
And here from gracious England have I offer
Of goodly thousands. But for all this,
When I shall tread upon the tyrant's head,
Or wear it on my sword, yet my poor country
Shall have more vices than it had before,
More suffer and more sundry ways than ever,
By him that shall succeed.'"
She closed the book and put her head down on the desk and cried.

Chapter 18

When Nettie returned home later that day, she went quietly into the kitchen and found her mother and Nana fixing dinner. She told them what had happened and said she wasn't hungry and went upstairs to her room and fell asleep, utterly exhausted. Her mother and Nana exchanged worried glances, but kept their fears to themselves.

Early the next day, a pounding was heard on the door. "What on earth?" wondered her mother out loud as she hurried to the front door, leaving Nettie standing over the sink. Nettie could hear her mother opening the door followed by loud German words. Nettie couldn't hear all of the words, but she froze, the dish cloth and ladle in her raised hands. The door leading to the living room swung open and there stood a German soldier with two more behind him. He stood there in the doorway, his beady eyes looking the petite woman up and down.

"Are you Bernadette Dupre?" he demanded.

"Yes," was all she could choke out.

"You are to come with me. You and Eulalie Dupre, your mother I believe."

"That is me," spoke up her mother from the other room.

"Good. Let's go." He ordered them out of their home and they all crammed into a waiting car. Nana stood helplessly on the porch, watching them go.

They drove swiftly in tense silence to Blanc Fleur and stopped before the building housing the Headquarters. They were ordered up the stairs and into the hall.

"Stay here," he barked to Nettie's mother and jerked Nettie by the elbow to the door leading to the Commandant's office. He opened it without knocking and shoved her inside.

Nettie stood there shivering, as they had been in such a rush to leave they had not had time to grab a coat to wear. She stood in front of the huge wooden desk and looked up to see Rolfe sitting in his chair. Behind him stood another officer; however, this one was not a typical soldier. Nettie knew from his black uniform and the lightening bolts, sometimes called 'daggers' attached to his collar, that he was one of the elite, a member of the SS.

Rolfe simply sat there, taking deep drags on a cigarette and blowing the smoke out into the room. What did she see in his eyes? Pity? The man behind him remained as unemotional as well, looking her up and down as the other soldier had done.

"May I ask what this is in regards to, Herr Commandant?" she asked, crossing her arms and trying to warm herself.

"It is an honor to see the girl who murdered Commandant Neumann," stated the unknown man sarcastically.

Uneasy and trying to keep her teeth from chattering, Nettie replied, "It was an accident. I thought the matter had been settled last year."

"Well, dear, it seems the name of Bernadette Dupre has reached the ears of the German Army yet again." he smirked.

"May I ask how?"

"Last week, in Dieppe, I was finally able to destroy a nest of the French Resistance that was sending radio messages across the channel."

Nettie shrugged. "I am still at a loss as to why you have dragged me here."

"It seems that in the barn they were using as their hideout there was a small oak barrel with the words 'Dupre's Calvados. Normandy' burned into it. Inside was quite a cache of electronic equipment. It didn't take us long to figure out that it was from the home of the infamous Mademoiselle Dupre of Blanc Fleur. Would you care to explain how your property ended up in Dieppe?"

Nettie hesitated while she tried to think of a lie, but then she realized that just maybe the truth would be the best answer. Most of the truth anyway. "It is true, the barrel and the equipment belong to me." Rolfe closed his eyes, but stayed silent. "My Uncle Jean-Paul operated the local electronics supply store here in Blanc Fleur. He died shortly before the war and my aunt asked if she could store the inventory at our farm because we had so much room." Nettie stopped to catch her breath before continuing. "I hid the items in the empty barrels and put them away. I was planning on selling the stuff after the war to help put the farm back on its feet." Tactfully Nettie had avoided mentioning that she had kept some of the supplies in the work shed.

"If it was hidden, how did these people find it? Did you sell it to them?" he questioned.

"No, I did not sell it or give it away. My family and I came back from town one day and it was missing."

"What day was that?" quietly asked Rolfe.

"It was during the Feast of All Saints. November 1st."

"Mademoiselle Dupre, it still doesn't answer how they knew it was there. Tell me right now *who knew* you even had the electronics?"

"I'm sure everyone in this town knew that the Dupre's had inherited the inventory. If nothing else, I have come to learn that in such a small town, everyone knows everyone else's business," Rolfe offered in a dismissive tone.

The other man glared at Rolfe and snapped, "I wasn't asking *you*, Commandant Wieber, I was asking *her*. And she had better come up with some names. ***Now!***"

Nettie stared at the floor for a moment and then raised her eyes and looked at Rolfe who sat silently once again. In a small voice she listed "My mother, grandmother, brother, sister, and my aunt Elita and her family knew. I don't know whom she may have told. Herr Commandant is right, everyone in Blanc Fleur may have known."

The man uttered an oath and reached for an envelope on the desk and took out some photographs. "Perhaps you recognize these people," he said as he flung them down on the desk in front of her. Nettie took a step forward and looked down at the half dozen photos. Seeing their contents, Nettie felt her stomach coming up into her throat. They showed several different people, both men and women, lying in the positions they must have fallen when they were shot. Some faces had been blown nearly completely off, but it was the last picture that Nettie slid out of the pile and glanced at that caught her attention. It showed the form of a young woman on her back in a pool of dark blood that nearly encircled the whole body. Her face, crowned by curly blonde hair, was untouched. While the features were more mature and thinner than the last time she had seem them, the resemblance to her father was unmistakable. It was Terese. Nettie looked up and started to say something, but in the next instant she found herself on the floor in the hallway.

She opened her eyes and found Frederick and her mother leaning over her. "Are you OK, dear?" soothed her mother as she rubbed Nettie's hands.

She reached up to stop the pounding of her head.

"You must have hit your head on the floor," commented Frederick.

"Mother." She tried to articulate, "Terese…"

"I know," she answered with tears in her eyes. "Frederick just told me."

"Pierre…is he in them too?"

"I will ask to see the pictures," she promised.

They could hear raised voices coming from the office and soon after it was flung open and Rolfe stood there in the doorway and sharply ordered Frederick to drive the Dupres home before shutting the door again and the voices resumed. Frederick picked Nettie up and carried her to the car. Her mother stayed behind, gathering up the courage to knock on the door and ask to see the pictures herself.

Nettie had just gotten settled in the back seat when her mother opened the car door and sat next to her daughter. She put her arm around Nettie and whispered, "I looked at the pictures and no, none of them is Pierre."

"I am sincerely happy to hear that, Madam Dupre," said Frederick from the driver's seat.

"I know you are, Frederick." She and Nettie spent the few minutes to their farm staring numbly out the windows.

Chapter 19

After the shock of finding out the fate of the youngest member of their family wore off, her mother set out to find out what facts she could. Because of the secrecy of the Resistance movement, there was little she could discover. What they did learn from kind citizens of the city of Dieppe was that the group had been operating out of the barn for a few weeks and had been preparing to move yet again when they had been discovered. They had all been killed in the shootout that followed, which was more of a comfort as the Dupres knew that any captured alive would have been tortured to give up any secrets they held, and then executed soon after. They could only guess that they had been right in believing that the small prints left behind in the mud had belonged to Terese herself, as she would have been one of the few who knew they had the supplies and where they were hidden. She must have guessed they would all have attended the All Saints Feast at the convent, as they had always attended that particular gathering.

Her mother made inquiries to find out where she had been buried and had received a reply from a kind priest that informed her that she had not had any identification on her and she had been placed in a mass grave. Perhaps after the war things could be rectified and her body reburied at Blanc Fleur.

The drabness of the weather reflected the Dupre household as the days passed by. Nettie did not go to town to meet with Rolfe, and he did not send for her. Oddly, even after the last meeting had ended, Nettie found herself missing the interaction between them. A week later, Adele knocked on their door. They welcomed her in and offered her some hot cider after her long walk from town. She warmed her hands on the hot mug for a moment before reaching into her pocket and pulled out a folded note and handed it to Eulalie.

She smiled and said, "I hope this will bring you good news."

Nettie's mother unfolded it and read it before reading it aloud. It said, "*I hope this finds you all well. I am sorry to report, if you do not know already, of the death of Terese. Trust that she died doing what she believed in, and would have had it no other way. I am fine, but cannot tell you any more for obvious reasons. I know I shall see you soon. Pierre.*"

"That is good news!" her mother stated. She folded the note back up and went into the kitchen to place the note in the wood burning stove.

"May I ask where you found that note?" asked Nana.

"It was on my bed at the convent when I went there for lunch. I asked Frederick if I could pay a social call on you since there wasn't much work to be done."

"How is your job going?" asked Nana.

"Fine, I guess." She looked troubled and continued, "Since you saw the Commandant last he has been keeping to himself in his office. He rarely speaks to Aimee and me. He seems withdrawn and I know you won't believe me, but Aimee even thinks he looks rather frightened. Of course, what a German would be frightened about, I have no idea."

"Is the SS officer still around?" asked Nettie.

"No, he left that same day. He didn't look at all happy, because I saw him stomp out of Headquarters and he and his men roared out of town. Aimee says she heard some of what was said and swears the SS officer told Rolfe that he was 'going to take note of this'. Of course, Aimee's German isn't very good."

They thanked Adele for coming all the way out to their farm and Nettie walked with her through the orchard to the back gate as Adele figured she might as well pay a visit to her own family while she was so close. Nettie waved goodbye and headed back to the house. She stopped by the distillery and opened its doors. Running her hands over the sturdy shelves and barrels, she wished she understood why her sister hadn't paid one last visit to her. Hadn't all those years been worth one last meeting? She had never had the chance to say goodbye. But maybe that is what Terese had been afraid of; afraid that if she had seen her family again, she wouldn't be able to leave the orchard. "I guess she had more important things to do than stay here," Nettie said to herself. "I wish I did." With that she walked back to the house and told her mother she wished to lie down, as she felt tired to the core of her being.

Nettie slept until the next day but did not feel any better and her chest was so constricted that she could barely catch her breath. Her mother felt her forehead and sent her back to bed. That evening she could barely breathe and the doctor was summoned from town. He announced that she had contracted pneumonia and left instructions for her care. By the following day her condition had worsened and she entered the fragile plain between life and death. Later, she wouldn't know what had caused her dreams and hallucinations—the illness or the medications.

In her deep haze, buried memories were uncovered and allowed to float free in her feverish mind. Some were pleasant, others not. At some time the memory that troubled her the most, yet was buried the deepest, came to the surface to haunt her. In it she was standing before the beehives in the yard behind the house. The day was sunny and warm and the bees buzzed lazily around her. She was dressed in a heavy canvas jumpsuit to protect herself, although the bees were usually extremely docile and rarely stung her; in fact she rarely wore the jumpsuit, but for some reason on this day she had decided to. She lifted the dripping combs from the hives and placed them in glass jars. A leering face came out of the fog and stood before her. He was talking but, in her dream, she couldn't hear what he was saying. She saw herself trying to gesture to him and indicate that it was not safe for him to stand so close to the hives. His hands reached out and tried to unzip the suit. She heard herself scream and, with her inborn instinct, push him away from her. He landed against an open hive, causing it to fall over and crash to the ground. Bees began to angrily buzz around them. He righted himself and slapped Nettie so hard across the face that her head snapped back. Tears stung in her eyes while a fury began to build up inside. She shoved him again, causing him to lose his balance and fall against another hive. Even more bees took to the air around them, filling the air with an angry hum. Screaming because the bees had begun to sting him, he swiftly got to his feet and grabbed the top off one of the hives and lifted it above his head, ready to crush the French woman's skull. Her arms instinctively flew up protectively. Out of the corner of her eye she saw a pair of arms reach out and give the Commandant a hard shove away from her. He fell backwards and landed squarely on yet another hive. With his backside he had broken through the top of the hive and was unable to get out. Horrible screams filled the air as he fought desperately to fight off the swarming insects. The same arms that had pushed the Commandant to his doom now grabbed her and together they ran to the house. From the window they watched as his legs kicked out spasmodically and the screams finally stopped.

It was only after the bees had calmed down and they had made certain that he was dead that Nettie and Frederick had their few stings attended to by a frightened Nana who asked, "What are you two going to do?"

Frederick answered, "He got too close to the hives. He fell, knocking them over. He died from the stings. Keep it short and simple." He then went back outside and dragged the body of his master to the car, placed it in the backseat, covered it with a blanket and drove back to town.

Within the hour they came for her. They took her to the ancient prison that stood in the center of town and locked her in one of the cells on the top floor. There she waited for questioning, which was not long in coming. She spent the entire night seated on a chair in the basement being questioned. She was slapped, beaten, and kicked, but her story never wavered. The Commandant had been careless, that was all. She did not see Frederick during this time but she did overhear two guards talking about him and indicating that he was in a cell below hers. Several days had passed of the same routine when she awoke on a hot, hazy June day to find a soldier standing over her.

"Get up. There is something for you to watch below." With that he turned on his heels and left. Her muscles were stiff and sore as she got up from her thin mattress that lay on the floor. Dried blood covered her face and arms. She heard voices coming from the small courtyard below her window and she stumbled over to the window to see what was happening. A man she did not recognize was waiting in front of the wall while a handful of soldiers holding rifles stood about twenty feet away. Another line of soldiers stood against another wall, well away from the action. It was one of these soldiers against the far wall that came forward and said something that she couldn't quite make out. At the time she hadn't thought much about that man who, it turned out, was in charge of ordering what came next. The unknown soldier walked over to the man standing alone next to the wall and offered him a blindfold. The man declined. The unknown soldier then stood clear as he ordered the men with rifles to aim and shoot. The violence of the war had swirled around her for the last four years, but the horror of having to watch it was too much as she went and threw up in a bucket in the corner of the cell.

It was soon after the execution that they came again for her. But rather than taking her to the basement, she went to a room that had been a sort of courtroom a century or two earlier. There were dozens of soldiers seated on benches around the large room. Nettie was led to the front and seated on a chair before a man who was apparently acting as a kind of judge. He looked at her, and after ordering silence from the onlookers, folded his hands before him and announced, "Mademoiselle Dupre, after questioning you and the German soldier who was also involved in the tragic death of Commandant Neumann, this court finds no fault with you or Frederick Von Allmon. You will both be released immediately. Do you have anything to say, Mademoiselle Dupre?"

Even though she was racked with pain, she was furious. This was no court! What right did they have to torture her? Common sense overtook her and she stated clearly and loudly, "No, I have nothing more to say."

"Then you are free to leave." And with that he brought down a gavel that he had probably stolen from a real courtroom. Nettie hesitated for a moment before standing up and walking slowly down the center aisle. She glanced to the right and to the left and ignored the insolent stares she was receiving. One man caught her eye. It was the same one who had offered the doomed prisoner a blindfold. His head was down and his cap was held in his hands. His hair was long and a shocking white blonde in color. His eyes then raised to watch the bedraggled woman in torn clothing make her way out of the courtroom. For a split second their eyes met, but a split second later she had to turn away from the dark gray eyes that looked into hers. She knew that face! It was only in her dream that she was able to replay that scene again and again. They had been Rolfe's eyes. In her delirium she gasped for breath as she realized what she had remembered. While that dream ended, others began. Phantoms flitted in her mind and gave her feverish mind no peace. Voices came to her in the darkness, but she could not respond.

It was early morning when she awoke. She looked around and found she was alone, which oddly was a relief to her. She sat up to get out of bed and found that it was a tremendous effort and decided to lie back down again.

Her mother soon looked in on her and a relieved look crossed her face when she saw her daughter awake and looking around. "Good morning, I was beginning to wonder about you." She touched her daughter's forehead and found that the fever had broken.

"How long have I been sick?" asked her patient weakly.

"About a week. You were pretty out of it. The doctor was worried."

"A week!" She found it disconcerting that so much time had passed without her knowledge. "Mother, did I have visitors while I was ill?"

Her mother seemed surprised that she would ask such a question, but answered, "Well, yes, you had several. Let's see, you had Anna and Adele, your Aunt Elita and Aimee, Father Bolet and Rolfe."

Nettie cringed at the last name. "Was I talking? When I was sick I mean?"

"Oh, yes. Nonsense really. You told Aimee that she was the prettiest kitten you had ever seen. She thought it was quite funny, you being so out of your mind." Nettie had a feeling her young cousin would not let her live *that* down. Then her mother cocked her head and added, "But it was really strange when Rolfe came by. You kept saying 'I know who you are' and something about a blindfold. I kept telling you that of course you knew who he was but Rolfe looked so ill at ease that he said he had to leave after a few minutes."

"He just left?"

"I am sure he just realized how sick you were and you needed your rest," she soothed, misunderstanding her daughter's question.

Nettie frowned and asked for something to drink. When her mother left on her errand, she reflected on her dream. Maybe her mind hadn't made it up after all, maybe she already knew. But what *did* she really know, *that* was the question.

March had just turned into April before Nettie was able to return to a normal routine. The school year had started back up the first week in March, but Nettie had had to leave the teaching in the capable hands of Marie-Claire. But the Sister had plenty of help when Rolfe had insisted that Adele and Aimee take leave from working with him and help out with the school. Aimee, on a visit to see her sick cousin, had told her that they rarely saw their boss, that he seemed preoccupied and anxious. She then added, "I know this sounds awful, and don't you tell anyone, but we miss him. He was nice and, well, he always gave us gifts."

Nettie laughed, commenting that it was the gifts they truly missed. When the girl had gone, she had to admit to herself that she knew exactly what they meant. She also decided she had to see him again, as much as the thought frightened her. But she hoped that if she saw him again, it would jog her memory and she would know if her dream had been revealing the truth or it had just been a dream.

She started back to work in the middle of April. She was excited to be back with her friends and be busy again. But her strength had not quite returned and she had to rest often. She liked to rest in Mr. LaPierre's warm office that overlooked the common courtyard. Watching the comings and goings of the soldiers kept her mind somewhat occupied. On one such day a long black car pulled into the courtyard, escorted by soldiers on motorcycles. Frederick ran down the steps to meet the car and swung open the back door and delivered a smart salute at the same time. The visitor was dressed in a dark overcoat and carried himself with authority. He followed Frederick up the stairs and disappeared into the building. Later, from the classroom, Nettie kept an eye on the car that was still parked in front of the entrance. About an hour after he had arrived the gentleman emerged, this time escorted by Rolfe. The visitor put his arm around the younger man's shoulder and gave him a gentle squeeze. With a final wave he stepped into the waiting car. Rolfe stood at attention as the car started up and headed out of the courtyard. Once the car was out of sight his shoulders stooped and, with head down, heheaded back into the building.

After class Nettie made up her mind to pay a call on Rolfe. She wanted to find out whom that man was and what such a person might be doing here in Blanc Fleur. She had not had the chance to see him close up since her illness. She would use the guise of re-starting the book club as the reason for her visit.

She made her way across the courtyard and after being waved through by a pair of soldiers playing cards, knocked on his door. She was rewarded with an unusually sharp "come in". She opened the door and stepped hesitantly into the room, shutting the door behind her. Rolfe was sitting in his chair with his booted feet propped up on the desk. He did a sluggish double take when he lifted his eyes to see who had disturbed him.

"I told them not to let anyone in."

"I guess they thought…"

"Don't tell me what they thought," he slurred. "Here, have a seat, Nett." He motioned with the hand occupied with a tumbler filled with amber liquid. Probably the same amber liquid that was in a bottle labeled 'whiskey' that sat half-empty on his desk. With the other hand he brought a cigarette to his lips and took a long drag and slowly exhaled, the gray smoke joining the hazy cloud hovering over his head. He flicked the ashes off onto the floor, which was just as well, as the silver ashtray was overflowing onto the papers scattered about. From his condition she correctly guessed that this party of one had been going on since his guest had left.

She gathered her nerves together and asked, "I was wondering, since I am back to work…and feeling better, did you want to start another book together?"

He gave her a long look through his bloodshot eyes and shook his head. "No, no…I am too busy. I don't think we can meet again," and with chilling finality added "ever."

She looked uneasily at him. In her heart she knew the answer to her question. She had seen him before. But what did it mean? He said nothing more; merely taking deep drags on the cigarette and a few gulps of whiskey. When she turned to leave, he called to her, "Be careful Nett, be careful." She looked back at him again and nodded slowly. Troubled, she walked down the stairs and made her way to Frederick's small office. The door was open but she knocked, which caused the young man to look up from his paperwork.

"Frederick, who was that man who visited this afternoon?"

"*That* man was Generalfieldmarschall Erwin Rommel himself."

"Rommel? Here? What did he want?"

"I thought you knew, Rommel and the Commandant's father are old friends. Rolfe has known him all his life. I suspect that is how he got the position here in Blanc Fleur."

"Yes. He did mention it before at the…" her voice trailed off. "Was it a social call? Rolfe seems very…ah…upset."

"I don't know what he wanted. He met with him in private. It was not a good meeting, I do know that."

"Thank you Frederick," and she started out the door.

"Ah Nettie," he hesitated.

"Yes Frederick?"

"I do hope you are better."

"Yes, I am. Thank you for asking." She smiled at the young man before she left the building, still pondering what the "Desert Fox" was doing in such an out-of-the-way place; surely he had more pressing matters.

Chapter 20

After her rather odd meeting with Rolfe, Nettie headed straight for the library to pick up her bicycle. While passing the door, she decided to pop in and say a quick hello to Lily. She opened the thick, ancient door and stepped inside. The dim hanging lights cast shadows about the interior. The high windows, meant for a church, allowed little light to filter in. Lily was nowhere in sight, so Nettie called her name and walked around, glancing down the aisles of wooden bookshelves.

"Behind you," said a quiet voice.

A startled Nettie jumped before turning around to face the librarian. "Lily, where were you?" she asked when she was able to catch her breath.

"Here." she answered casually. "What can I help you with?"

"I just wanted to say hello. I haven't been in for so long because I was ill. I wanted to thank you for recommending those books for me that you gave to my mother."

"Yes, I heard that you were very ill. Your mother came in often to find books for you. I think it's the most I have seen her in town in years. I was worried when I saw you because I thought you were going to tell me my children were acting up in school."

Nettie shook her head. "Oh no. Dom and Rene are doing very well in their studies. I guess Dom will be in my class next year. I'm looking forward to that." Looking up at one of the narrow windows she added, "Well, it looks like it will be dark before we know it. I had better start home."

"Don't make yourself a stranger, Nett," Lily called after her.

Nettie could hear Lily lock the door after her when she departed the building. It was so strange, where had Lily been? The library wasn't that large. Perhaps she had been on the floor behind the circulation desk, but why hadn't she returned her greetings? The sight of a red ribbon tied to her bicycle interrupted her thoughts about Lily. It had been months since the last ribbon had been left for her, which was just as well because of the shortage of parts she had available. She untied the ribbon and stuffed it in to her coat pocket. She made haste pedaling home as she was already an hour late and didn't wish to worry her mother and Nana.

She was tired when she got home, still not totally recovered from her bout with pneumonia. She ate dinner and then rested on the davenport until later in the evening. When the clock struck 9 o'clock she slipped out the door and made her way to the clearing, staying off the path. For some reason she hesitated at the edge of the clearing. She felt unsettled, was it because of the strange meetings she had had? Or was she just tired? Hearing nothing, she advanced into the clearing and crept to the cistern and lifted the heavy lid. She set the lid on the grass and reached in to lift out what may have been left for her. To her utter shock she touched warm, human flesh. A scream escaped from her lips as she jumped back. A man appeared before her eyes from the depths of the cistern. From the light of the moon she could see that he was frantically waving his arms and in a voice barely above a whisper he was saying "Hush…please don't talk.shhhh."

Nettie turned and was sprinting toward the trees when she heard "Bernadette! Bernadette!" She entered the tree line and stopped. The leaves had not sprung to life on their bare limbs, but the branches were thick enough to hide her in the darkness. She could make out the figure climbing out of the cistern. He stumbled in her general direction, still calling her name. What should she do?

She stepped out of the trees and ordered, "Stop right there," and he obeyed.

He spoke next. "Bernadette? It is you isn't it?"

"Yes," she answered.

"I need your help. Someone said you could help me."

"Who are you? What do you want?" she demanded, realizing that while he was speaking French fluently it was with an accent she did not recognize.

My name is Jacque and I am from Quebec. Please, that is all that I can tell you."

"How did you get here? How did you know about the cisterns?"

He remained silent for a moment before he said, "I can't really tell you how I got here, but I have something in the cistern that may explain better than I can about how I came to be in there."

He made his way back to the cistern and gently pulled out a large bundle. He held it up and unwrapped it before her. It was a radio; a radio made out of silver and mahogany.

"How did you get that?" she asked.

"I was walking along the road back there," he motioned to the back road, "and I ran into a German who led me here, told me to wait for you and then told me to give you this. He said you would know who it belonged to."

"What did he look like?"

"Tall, young, red-haired. Do you know him?"

"Oh yes, I know him," she answered grimly. How could he put this total stranger in her cistern? Who was he really?

"Are you hungry?" she inquired.

"Starved."

She looked him up and down before saying, "Stay here in the trees and keep your ears open. I'll go get you some food, blankets, and fresh clothing and be right back. Here, give me the radio." She tucked the radio under her arm and made her way cautiously to the work shed where she tucked the radio in the floor hiding space. Anxious expressions greeted her when she entered the side door into the kitchen.

"Did you retrieve another radio?" asked her mother.

"Yes. In fact it is Rolfe's radio again. And you'll never guess what else Frederick left with the radio."

"What?" asked Nana curiously.

"A Canadian."

"What!?" they exclaimed in unison.

Nettie went on to tell them what had happened at the cistern. The three of them then prepared a bundle of supplies for their unexpected guest. Nettie then made her way back to the edge of the clearing and found the Canadian leaning against a tree.

She handed him the bundle with the advice, "You'll be safer in the cistern. I have reason to believe the Germans patrol this orchard frequently. I included a flashlight. Only use it if you have to."

"OK," he agreed as he climbed back into the cistern.

"Keep this lid in place as much as possible. I'll bring more supplies and check on you tomorrow."

"Thank you. I'll see you then," he replied as he helped her slide the top back into place.

She made her way back to the house deep in thought. What was she going to do with this stranger? Unlike a radio, she couldn't hide him forever. Who could she trust to approach about helping him? Obviously the Colliers had help when they disappeared. She knew talking to the wrong person would be disastrous to her and this person she was hiding.

Later as she climbed into bed she had a thought. She would talk to Frederick. Since he knew about her radio service, she had a feeling he also knew about other things. Plus, he had been the one to direct the man to hide there in the first place, so asking him would not be dangerous.

The next morning, Nettie ate a quick breakfast and told her mother and Nana the idea she had come up with and requested that they stay away from the clearing until she had gotten him safely far away.

She pedaled into town much earlier than usual and rode into the school courtyard and looked for Frederick among the other soldiers milling outside the barracks. His red hair was easy to spot and she called out to him.

He walked over to her and greeted her with a "Guten Morgen Fraulien Dupre. When he was close to her and out of earshot of the others he asked, "Did you get my package?"

She looked up at the smiling youth and in a low voice demanded, "What were you thinking? What am I supposed to do with him?"

Frederick smiled back. "You! What was I going to do with the man? Hide him in the Commandant's desk?"

Nettie huffed, "Frederick, answer me this. Why didn't you shoot a stranger you met on the back road in the middle of the night?"

"It would be rather difficult, since my pistol isn't loaded."

"And the Commandant knows this?"

"I see no reason to burden him with my beliefs."

"I believe that you are required to answer to him."

"Nettie, I know that someday I will answer to Him, and my conscience will be clear." She looked at him and tried to understand what he was saying. Giving up on that for the moment she asked, "What am I supposed to do with him?"

"Well, I hear confession is good for the soul."

"Frederick!" she sputtered. Then she lowered her voice when she realized that the other soldiers were watching them. "Frederick, please stop kidding."

"I'm not kidding, confession is good for the soul," he repeated as he turned around and milled with the other soldiers who were making their way into Headquarters for another day at work.

Confession! She thought to herself. Oh, of course! She huffed again. Why didn't he say so? She turned her bike around and rode over to Marie-Claire who was walking toward the school.

She pulled up beside her friend. "Marie, I'll be late. I have to see Father Bolet for confession."

"That's great Nett." remarked Marie-Claire.

Nettie didn't answer and pedaled off to the nearby church. A few stragglers were still making their way out of the door from morning Mass when she arrived and parked her bicycle. The penitents were seated in the front pew and Nettie took her seat at the end of the row. She could hardly breath, her heart raced, and getting more nervous by the moment.

A late arriving parishioner took a seat next to her and she looked over to see that it was old Madam Derauseaux who was the mother of the town butcher. Nettie leaned over and whispered into her ear, "Please go ahead of me, I may take awhile." The old woman opened her eyes wide and looked at her in amazement. "And I had always thought of you as *such a nice girl*, Bernadette."

Nettie opened her mouth and found that she was actually speechless. Instead she just stood up and moved to the other side of the old woman.

At last it was her turn. She slowly stood up and entered the little box. She closed the curtain behind her, but then reconsidered and opened them a crack so that she could see if anyone entered the church. For now the coast was clear. She could hear the priest on the other side of the grate, probably wondering what this person was doing.

"Is someone there?" he finally asked.

"Yes, I...need to talk to you Father." She croaked, hoping he didn't recognize her voice.

"Go on, that is why I am here," he assured her.

"I need something ...*I need something* ...picked up."

"I don't understand," was his reply. "What do you need picked up?"

"Father, I have a man I need picked up. I need a man moved from where he is now and I have reason to believe that he needs to go somewhere in particular."

"Where does he need to go?"

"I don't know, he wouldn't tell me. But he needs to be moved from where he is now."

"I take it he is alive."

"Oh yes."

After a pause the priest asked, "Where is he now?"

"He is in o...er, he is hiding in one of the cisterns in the orchard on the Dupre farm. Do you know what I am talking about?" Of course Nettie knew he had been to their farm on numerous occasions, but she couldn't let on that she knew *that*, could she?

"Yes, I know how to get there. When should I come for him?"

"Soon as possible, please."

"I will come for him one night this week; he must be ready to go at a moment's notice."

"Yes, Father." With those words she slipped out of the confessional and sprinted out the nearest exit. She mounted her bicycle and fled to the library to leave her bicycle there in the back garden.

Nettie was considerably late when she finally walked into the classroom. Later, Marie-Claire murmured to her, "Do you feel better?"

"Much!" was her heartfelt reply. The nun smiled at the news and Nettie didn't have the heart to tell her the truth.

The rest of the day dragged on and all Nettie could think about was the man in the cistern. Being caught with radios was one thing; hiding a person who was obviously wanted by the Germans was quite another. The dismissal bell rang at last and since she no longer met with Rolfe she could head straight home. She had glanced toward his office several times that day and all she could make out was the back of the rocking chair going forward and back.

She found her mother and Nana sitting on the porch swing waiting for her. "What's wrong?"

"Nothing," assured her mother. "We are just relieved that it turned out to be you coming down the road. We had to quickly hide him in the cellar."

Nettie didn't bother to ask who "he" was. They must have snooped around the clearing after she told them specifically not to. She sat down on the porch railing and told them what she had arranged for him and hoped to have him picked up that week. She went up-stairs to relax and when she came down for dinner she found Jacques seated at the table.

Her mother noticed the look on her daughter's face and defended herself with the statement, "I thought we could give him one good meal before he had to go. They won't come looking for him until after dark anyway."

Nettie acquiesced and took her place at the table. While they ate she told him of the plan that had been put in place. Having been cut off from most of the world for nearly four years and hearing only what the Germans wanted them to hear, they pumped this young man for information on how the war was really going and things from ordinary life that had disappeared from Normandy years ago.

Although he couldn't talk about how he happened to be in Normandy and why, he was free to talk about anything else and he did. He talked about Quebec and the Cathedral De Notre Dame, the sidewalk cafés. Nettie commented that it sounded much like Paris, years ago anyway.

He said that he had been to the tiny town of Callander and seen for himself the identical quintuplets that had been born there in the 1930's. "Its true, five identical girls, the cutest things you have ever seen." He also talked about the struggle of the French to hang onto their culture in an English Commonwealth. Nettie was tempted to inform him that many in the providence of Brittany considered themselves English and indeed English was the native language of many of them, but she held her tongue. Nettie inquired if he had any knowledge of Louis, but he had not heard of him.

Later, Nettie stood restlessly by the kitchen window, waiting for darkness to come so it would be safe to deliver Jacques back to the cistern. Finally, she called him from the living room where he had been talking to her mother and Nana and they left from the side door. She stayed off the main path and directed him through the trees. The night was pitch black as the clouds blotted out the moon. For some reason the orchard frightened her that night. It was mid-May and the apple blossoms were thick and fragrant on the trees. During the day, never would one see or smell a more beautiful sight than that of hundreds of apple trees in full bloom. As they made their way through the trees, the wind shook the branches and white petals floated eerily down around them. When they reached the edge of the clearing, she stopped and listened for several moments. Hearing nothing but the wind in the trees, she pushed her fears to the back of her mind and led Jacques back to the cistern and lifted the lid. He climbed in and she slid the lid back into place and carefully made her way to the tree line. Something didn't feel right, so she couched down and lay flat on her stomach under a tree and waited. The petals rained softly around her as she listened. She was just about to rise back up again when she thought she heard a soft rustling sound coming from the other side of the clearing, but perhaps it was her imagination working overtime, or perhaps it was the priest coming to get Jacques.

So sudden did the shouting and shooting erupt that she was on her feet and running before she could better assess the situation in which she found herself. She swerved to catch a little used path home when, in the darkness, she ran head on into a man. His arms enveloped her to keep her from falling and his gloved hand covered her mouth to prevent her from calling out in surprise. In her confusion, her arms encircled the dark form. The wool of an overcoat scratched her cheek. The scent of expensive cologne filled her nostrils. Her arms answered instinctively and reached out to push him away and continue on her flight. His arms relaxed, letting her go.

She raced up the side steps to the kitchen and the door opened before she could reach for the knob. "Here, put this on," ordered her mother. Together they stripped off her dark clothing and Nettie slipped a long nightgown over her head as her mother stuffed her clothing in a ragbag and stuffed it into a closet. Nettie reached back and untied her braid as they ran up the steps and joined Nana at the top of the stairs, looking out a window that overlooked the orchard.

"There!" Nana whispered nervously, "Some are coming to the house." She pointed to a bobbing light heading from the orchard to the back of their house. Nettie slumped to the floor and hugged her knees. She could still feel the rough wool against her cheek and smell the spicy musk of his expensive cologne. Along with her mother and Nana she waited for the knock on the door that was not long in coming. Nana made her way down the steps and opened the door. Several soldiers pushed their way in and began to search the house. Nettie and her mother were ordered down the stairs to stand next to Nana near the door. With dismay and fear they watched the men paw through their belongings. It was during this melee that Rolfe entered the house and looked at the three women. His hand reached up and snatched something from Nettie's hair. He then turned around and called to someone outside. "They're in here."

The same SS officer that had questioned her in February and so cruelly informed her of her sister's murder walked through the door. His cold eyes settled on Nettie as he spoke to Rolfe. "Herr Commandant, surely you will bring this woman in to town with us and have her shot when the sun comes up."

"I am sorry to disagree, Strumbannfurer. As you can see for yourself, these women were just wakened up. Obviously they cannot be responsible for everything that goes on in their orchard."

He looked at the women in their nightclothes and sat down before speaking. "I am sorry to have to inform you that Father Bolet was shot to death in your orchard this evening."

The three women gasped and clutched each other in genuine shock. After ordering the soldiers out, the man turned on his heels and left. Rolfe then spoke up. "We had information that a paratrooper had gone down in the area two nights ago. The SS has been suspicious about your priest for some time and followed him here. The paratrooper got away, the good Father was not so fortunate. We will be keeping a close eye on this area until he is apprehended." With that he raised his fist and opened it to reveal two white flower petals. He looked at her and echoed his earlier words, "Be very careful, Nettie," and left.

Chapter 21

The next day dawned cold and dreary. To Nettie it was like watching someone else move around the house as she dressed, ate breakfast, and left for work. Before stepping over the threshold of the front door, she was stopped by the sight of two shriveled petals that had fallen where he had dropped them the night before. She reached down and, picking them up, threw them out the door.

What should she do now? Should she run, like the Colliers? She thought about her mother and Nana. She had doubts they could survive such a venture, especially Nana. Leaving on her own would endanger them. With deep sadness she realized she was just back to where she began, trapped in Blanc Fleur.

When she pedaled into town she found the streets nearly deserted. She rode to the library and noticed the 'Closed' sign was still up on the door. On a hunch she walked to the church to see if word had reached the Sisters yet. She found nearly the whole town milling around outside the church or trying to make their way inside.

"Oh Nett!" she heard a sob behind her. It was Clea. "Have you heard?"

"I know. He was shot in my orchard." a numb Nettie responded.

Clea's eyes opened wide in disbelief, "In *your* orchard? What happened out there last night Nett?"

Nettie stared blankly back. "He was helping me and…Oh Clea! He died because of me!" Her sobs shook her body as she doubled over. Clea put her arms around her and ushered her into a deserted alley and they sat on the back stoop of a shop.

"Tell me what happened, Nett."

In a muted voice Nettie told her the story of finding the Canadian in the well, and except for leaving out Frederick's role in the story, told her everything that had happened up through Rolfe removing the incriminating petals from her hair. "So you see, he would not have been there without me asking him for help. It's all my fault."

Clea gently shook her with both hands and said, "No, Nett, it wasn't *because* of you, it was *because* of this war. It was the war and what it has done to everyone that killed him. *They* killed him. Someday you will know that." Nettie looked at her, wanting to believe her. Maybe someday she would, but not on that day. Clea went on, "You have made yourself a powerful ally in the Commandant, Nett."

Anger built up in Nettie as she turned to her friend and declared, "He is not my friend, Clea. I hate that man, really I do."

Clea didn't answer, but reached into her pocket and pulled out a clean handkerchief "Come, dry your tears so you can cry some more at the church," sniffled Clea. They made their way back to the front of the church and waited in line to enter through the front doors. After some time they reached the altar area and found the priest laid out on a table that Nettie knew had come from the Convent dining room. The Sisters sat in a semi circle around the body. Nettie thought the priest looked peaceful, probably for the first time since the war came to Blanc Fleur. Marie-Claire caught sight of them and rose from her chair and made her way to a corner in the front of the church and waited until Nettie and Clea had paid their respects.

She hugged them both and proceeded to tell the women what had transpired the evening before. It seemed that the Commandant had knocked on their door and summoned Philippe, the handy man, to help him retrieve the body from his car and place him in the church. Then they had moved a table from the dining room to the church and placed the body on it. It was then that he had ordered the Sisters to come to the common room and told them what had happened and apologized. She finished with the words, "and then that poor man turned and left."

Nettie and Clea looked at each other but didn't say anything; Marie-Claire hadn't looked so grieved since the death of Sister Paula.

They left by way of a side door and circled around to the front of the church. An arm reached out of the crowd and stopped Nettie. She was astounded to see it was Rolfe. He looked down at her and in a low menacing voice he warned, "The priest was a good man, but he was very foolish. Don't be foolish Nettie." With that said, he let her go and went up the church steps. "I am so sorry," expressed Frederick. He looked exhausted and there were dark circles under his eyes. "Thank-you, Frederick," answered Clea as she gently squeezed his arm before he followed his master inside.

Clea and Nettie headed to the school where a few children had gathered for school that day. They were subdued; granted they had become used to tragedy, but the death of the much loved parish priest was hard to explain to children, to anyone.

Later, as Nettie tried to explain the day's lesson, she was interrupted by Henri-Claude who asked, "Is that thunder?"

Nettie cocked her head and answered, "No, the allies must be bombing nearby. It's odd they're bombing during the day. Well, we wish them the best don't we?"

"Will they bomb us?" Henri-Claude asked nervously. The others listened with rapt attention.

"I doubt it, Henri. They want to wipe out the train lines, bridges, and ports. We don't have anything here that is worth destroying."

A little girl named Giselle raised her hand.

"Yes, Giselle?" prompted Nettie.

The girl screwed up her face and asked, "Mademoiselle Dupre, aren't those *our* bridges, trains, and ports they are bombing?"

Even Nettie had to smile. "Well, while the Germans are still here, nothing belongs to us. So the answer Giselle is yes and no. But back to the original question, I am sure we are quite safe from the bombers here in Blanc Fleur."

As she turned back to the board and started to write the day's spelling words on the board she thought to herself that Henri had brought to her attention that the Allies had increased in the number of bombing raids. That was a good sign, and she had seen a decrease in the number of luftwaffen planes she had seen flying overhead.

After school she walked her bicycle through the streets as they were filled with people who had come to pay their respects to the Sisters. They had also come to hear the details of what exactly had happened the night before. Some looked at Nettie out of the corner of their eyes and turned away if she looked directly at them; others came and paid their condolences. Nettie was relieved to reach the town gates and leave all this behind her, at least for the night. Just as she mounted her bicycle she heard someone softly calling her name. She looked behind her and at first did not see anyone. She was about ready to leave when she heard it again. She led her bicycle back toward the wall and found Frederick hiding in the shadows.

"I am so sorry, Nett, I didn't mean for this to happen…"

"I know," she interrupted. "I already know that Frederick. But please tell me why. Why did you help him, you didn't have to. You put on a show in front of your own people to make them think you are stupid and clumsy. Why? You're supposed to be the enemy, or haven't you noticed?"

He looked to be near tears. "I know everyone wonders why I am still a lackey after four years. Why I screw up everything. The truth is I want to stay in my lowly position, run errands, drive cars, and organize the Commandant's schedule. This way I know I will never see any action on the front. I can't be like the rest of them because I am a mitglied der gesellschaft der Freude."

"What? A member of the Society of Friends? What *are* you talking about?" she asked in an exasperated tone.

"I am a Friend."

"Of course you're a friend, Frederick, but what…"

"No, Nett. It means that I am a *Friend*, a Quaker." He half smiled. "The Germans don't care too much for people who will not take arms against others, either. My family is very active, albeit underground Quakers in Berlin. They have worked for years to stop what is happening in Germany and several have been exiled or worse. I had to join up because of my age and gender and to throw suspicion off my parents and older sisters. My father was able to arrange for this post to keep me out of the action. We never thought the war would go on for this long. It has not been easy but I can say that I have not deserted my faith."

"But what about last summer?" Nettie asked as she reached out to the shaking youth.

"I have searched my conscious and I wouldn't change what I did, Nett. I am not sorry I saved you, how could I be? I am not sorry I lied to my own people—well, that's a laugh isn't it? My *people* wouldn't drag other human beings off to camps, shoot them in the streets because of their religious or political beliefs." Looking at her startled face he went on, "Oh yes, its all true. The stories of those camps—that's quite a word for them isn't it? My parents and sisters have assured me it is all true and worse than a person can imagine." He was quite hysterical now and Nettie shushed him, fearing they would attract attention of passers-by.

He slowly calmed down. "I am so sorry Nett. I know you have your own troubles with the orchard, your sister. I didn't know what else to do. I had no idea that the SS knew about it. They came to see Rolfe late yesterday afternoon; I was already off duty and didn't find out what had happened until the Commandant returned. He said that the SS soldiers were the ones who shot the priest and the parachutist escaped. I never would have forgiven myself if something had happened to you. I feel so bad over the priest…"

Nettie looked down at her feet. It would not serve any purpose to tell him that she had indeed been caught and for whatever reason, released.

Frederick squeezed her hands in his and said, "I know it will all be over soon." And then he turned and disappeared into the shadows of the town wall. Nettie mounted the bicycle and was just about to push off when she caught sight of Rolfe leaning against the wall of a nearby building. He stood there watching her, leisurely smoking a cigarette. She regained her composure and pretended she had not seen him and rode off as quickly as she could. He did not call out to her.

Chapter 22

The next morning the Dupre women ate a simple breakfast of toast and apple butter washed down with weak coffee in silence. Each was reflecting on the events of the last three days and how close disaster had come to each of them. Mechanically they went about the morning chores before changing into their best clothes and heading out the door. Along the road into town, they merged with other mourners. Their conversations were subdued, even all the destruction they had witnessed over the last four years had not prepared them for the violent end of the village priest.

Side by side they marched into the church and squeezed into the pews or stood along the pillars and walls. Benches and chairs had been tucked into any available space. Nettie's mother and Nana found the first they came to, toward the back. Nettie shuffled forward and found a seat next to Anna and her family.

She had just sat down when the person to her left was suddenly ordered up and Rolfe took his place next to a stunned Nettie.

"What are you doing here?" she hissed through clenched teeth.

"I have come to pay my respects. I consider myself a member of this community too," he answered evenly.

"Really? I took you for the man who murdered him," she muttered under her breath.

Anna poked her in the ribs, this was not the time or place for this conversation. For the next hour she listened to the priest from a neighboring town give the funeral mass. As his words ran on, Nettie gazed up at the stained glass windows of the ancient church. She had looked at them a million times over the entire thirty-four years of her life. She had been baptized here, had her first communions and confessions, had even been confirmed here. And like the majority of the residents of Blanc Fleur, planned on having their funerals here. But she had never really *looked* at the pieces of colored glass arranged to tell a story in each of the windows. She looked at the large window to the right of the altar. In the depicted scene, Joan of Arc knelt at the base of a large apple tree, undoubtedly praying for guidance in how to push the English across the Channel. Nettie thought it ironic that most of these people gathered in the church that morning were praying the English would come. How times had changed! Her attention was drawn back to the service as a few of the Sisters and some members of the parish got up to say a few words about their deceased friend and spiritual leader. A few of the speakers glanced in the Commandant's direction, and not surprisingly, no one mentioned the manner in which he had died. Out of the corner of her eye she examined the man next to her. His dark blonde hair was carefully slicked back; the nails of the hands set calmly in his lap were clean and clipped short. The uniform, while slightly worn, was freshly pressed, the boots polished to a black shine. It occurred to her that he had taken great care in his appearance. To take her mind off the proceedings before her and the man next to her, she looked back up at the window once again. The large gnarled apple tree seemed to embrace the praying girl. In the background was a large, stocky gray horse whose head was bent toward its rider, the young Joan. His head appeared almost comical, as if he was trying to overhear her prayers. Nettie wished the horse could tell her what magical words she uttered. What words had she received from God that had led her and the French people to drive the English out? Would they work on the Germans, she Wondered? Joan herself was dressed in a rather dull, gray armor, her short, cropped head bent over clasped hands. She was forever in prayer, this Joan of the window. Nettie dropped her eyes to the handkerchief in her lap. Perhaps prayers like Joan's would no longer work. Surely God was tired of stopping wars humans had started.

She glanced again at the man beside her. This time she studied his face, which was bowed. A tired and sad expression was evident on his features. For an instant she felt sorry for him, but that quickly dissipated and anger build up inside her. Why was he unhappy? He didn't have that right. It was him and his kind that had murdered the priest, Terese, Sister Paula, and had taken over their lives for the last four years. He didn't deserve her pity or anything else. She jumped to her feet as the congregation began the ending hymn. Her movement was so sudden that Rolfe had looked down at her. She looked him straight in the eyes with such a furious look in her eye that startled him so much he dropped his hymnal onto the pew ahead of him and it landed with a sharp "thump" that caused the surrounding people to look around. After the processional of the priest had passed, Rolfe abruptly excused himself and left via the center aisle. The still singing parishioners watched the visibly shaken Commandant make his way out of the church.

A few minutes later the congregation made their way out of the church. The priest would be buried later with just the Sisters and a few members of the pastoral staff attending. There was nothing to do but go home.

The next day being Saturday was a day of rest, at least for the students. But for the adults, the work during the spring never seemed to end. After several cool and damp days, the sun that greeted them on that Saturday was especially welcomed. Her mother and Nana were busy planting in the garden and Nettie, not really caring for garden work, decided to look elsewhere for work that needed to be done. She walked out into the back yard, near the tree line and poked around the hives. With the apple trees still in bloom, the hives were literally humming with life. She placed her hands on the sides of one of the hives and could feel the vibrations of hundreds of thousands of tiny, beating wings. In a few days she would need to harvest the honey to make room for even more honey production.

With a gentle pat on the side of the hive she made her way into the trees and walked to the work shack. Pulling the key out of her pocket, she opened the locked door and went inside, not bothering to shut it behind her. She opened the windows to let in the mild air and sunlight. After she had leaned against the workbench and relaxed for a few more moments, she knelt down and pried up the board that hid the compartment under the floor. She reached in and pulled out the Commandant's radio. The sooner this was repaired and out of her sight, the better. She set it on the workbench and opened the back to allow her to look at the insides. One of the tubes was definitely burned out and she removed it. She opened the hidden cupboard and compared the tube to the few remaining ones on her shelves. One looked to be a match and she fit it in the empty space and found that it fit. She plugged it in and turned the silver "on" knob and was relieved to hear a tune playing. She tuned the station in and, enjoying the music, turned the volume up.

The catchy tune coupled with the warm breeze caused her to poke her head out the back window to breath in deeply the scent of the apply blossoms emanating from the orchard. Her eyes were closed as she breathed in the fresh, fragrant scent.

Without warning, the music stopped. Nettie opened her eyes and turned around. It was the Commandant. He stood there staring at her, no expression in the gray eyes that had become cold. After a few uneasy moments he snapped, "Is my radio ready for pick-up?"

Horror rushing through her body, she knew that there was to be no escape from her carelessness. She had begun to back up slowly when his arm whipped out and he grabbed her long braid of hair. Her feet left the ground as he threw her out of the shack with one yank. She landed on the ground with a loud thud. She looked up at the twisted face she no longer recognized. Twenty feet to her right she glimpsed the hives, teeming with bees that were already on heightened alert because of the altercation taking place so close to their homes. Could she make it? She looked back at him again, his hair falling over his red face and bulging eyes. In two steps he came to stand over her and he sneered, "You stupid girl!" She caught the following words between his pounding fists upon her prone body, her arms over her head. "I just wanted to get out of here! You couldn't stay out of the way, could you?" All she could do was stay on the ground and cover her head. As his arms tired, she let down her arms and scooted herself toward the hives. The bees began to hum with alarm at the perceived danger. If she could only knock it over, perhaps it would all be over, just like last time. He stopped beating her and was bending over, breathing hard. She stumbled to her feet and ran the last few feet to the hives. Quick as a cat, he grabbed her by the collar of her work shirt and held her above the ground, her feet kicking helplessly.

"It was no accident, *was it? Was it?*" he shouted into her face.

She stopped her struggle and looked into his gray eyes and said simply, "No, it was not an accident."

With that he dropped her and hit her about the head and face. She did not try to protect herself. Now that he knew the truth there would be no escaping. Now that she had said it out loud there was no hiding from herself. She wanted to die. Her body relaxed and her ears buzzed in the most peculiar way and she floated into blackness.

She vaguely remembered deep sobbing and heavy steps retreating from her. Her mother's face loomed above hers, mouthing words she could not hear. Darkness again crept over her and that was all she remembered until she awoke in a bed during the night. Was it the same night? She wasn't sure. It took her a moment to realize that she was in her grandmother's bed. A light snore came from a chair near her. She could make out the sleeping form of her mother, keeping watch over her daughter. The room began to spin and her ears buzzed as before and she drifted away again.

Her next memory was of Dr. Boyce leaning over her and shining a light into her eyes. Her mother and Nana seemed relieved at what he was saying to them, although Nettie could barely hear a word. They left the room and she tried to remember why she was in bed and was sore all over. Had the pneumonia returned? No, she decided. After a few minutes the fog in her mind lifted somewhat and images slipped back into her consciousness. She remembered the bees…had they killed Rolfe? Why did that thought frighten her? No, Rolfe had walked away after beating her. It was what she as a murderer deserved, she rationalized. She had led him to believe that she was only an innocent observer of the events that took place in Blanc Fleur and he had protected her only to discover that she had committed the most heinous of crimes, and worst of all had never felt a pang of guilt. She had become one of *them*, she decided, that is why Rolfe had let her live. She rolled over; she wanted the next best thing to death, sleep.

For several days she stayed in bed, asking them to leave her alone. It was while she was alone that the sun filtering into the room awakened her. She sat up in bed and glanced at the mirror hanging over the wash basin. She slipped out from between the sheets and made her way unsteadily towards it. She hung onto the dresser underneath the looking glass and, with some trepidation, took a closer look at her reflection. She never could have been prepared for the sight that greeted her. The many bruises were in full bloom, making her face a patchwork of blue, green and yellow. Her lip was cut in several places and a large cut graced her forehead. She suddenly hated the empty shell standing before her and grabbed a pair of shears laying on the dresser. She began cutting the first thing she could reach, her hair. The brown tresses fell into piles onto the wooden floor. With her energy spent, she looked at her reflection again. In her confused mind she didn't recognize the new face staring back at her and she rationalized that no one else would recognize her as the murderer she was. She fell back into bed and back into a deep sleep.

The following week she was strong enough to sit outside. Her mother clipped at what was left of her hair as she sat on an old stool. Nettie had been delirious and out of her head when she cut her hair, her mother reasoned away any inquiries visitors had put forth.

"I guess you should go see Aimee. Elita says she has a natural talent for working with hair. I think I am just making it worse."

"No, it's fine mother." She looked in the mirror and saw the short pageboy her mother had sculptured out of what was left of her hair.

"You look just like I did when I was little," smiled her mother.

"Great. I'm so glad the style has stayed the same." She arose from her stool and strolled into the orchard. The blossoms were almost gone now, the grass littered with the brown, rotting petals. She found it comforting now to walk amongst the familiar trees and mused that perhaps she would take over the care of the orchard. She walked to the distillery and let herself in. She breathed deeply of the sharp scent of apple brandy that lingered in the air. She took a seat on an empty barrel and lost herself in the moment.

A few minutes later she heard a voice calling her name. She stiffened. Who was it? In another moment she recognized it as a woman's voice. She stood up and went to the door. A figure strode down the path toward her, and seeing Nettie standing there, waved. It was Clea. Her friend must have talked to Nana or her mother, as she made no comment on her new hairstyle or the slight bruises still evident on her face.

Clea gave her a big hug and said, "I have been so worried, Nett." She then stopped and took a closed look at her friend's face and added, "I heard rumors of what happened; they were true, weren't they?"

Nettie nodded and told her what had happened and finished with the statement, "I wish he had killed me, Clea. I have become one of them."

Her friend protested but Nettie cut her off. "I murdered Commandant Neumann. I did. He was an evil man, but after I did it, I never felt guilty. Not for a second." Her shoulders slumped over.

"Oh Nett. I know what happened to Commandant Neumann. I have known since last summer."

"You weren't there." she responded dully. Then a thought crossed her mind "Frederick told you. Didn't he?"

Clea nodded and said, "Yes, he told me Nett. Frederick tells me a lot of things…and I tell Frederick a lot of things. I wish I had known how you felt about it, I would have talked to you long ago. But with our vow of never talking about what we do, *what we have to do*, Nett, I didn't dare ask you about it. As for you being like one of them, you'll never be. If you were truly evil Nett, you would have killed Rolfe, but your feelings for him saved him. And like it or not, his feelings for you saved you."

"I hate him."

"No you don't."

"But I do. He is one of them. They killed our friends and family. Ruined…everything," insisted Nettie.

Clea shook her head. "Someday. Someday soon we will talk."

"Say whatever it is now."

"No. After all is over." She smiled and squeezed Nettie's hand. "We will when we crack open Francois's bottle of 'Dupre's finest'. It won't be long Nett. The bombing by the Allies is increasing. The tide is turning."

Nettie shook her head sadly. She felt that it was too late for her.

Clea sighed at not being able to convince her friend. "Nett, I need to ask you something else."

"What?"

"Have you seen Frederick recently? He seems to be…gone."

"What do you mean gone?"

"A few weeks ago we noticed he wasn't around. It seemed to be about the same time as…"

"Rolfe paid his visit to me?"

"Yes," Clea nodded. "And Chat says she saw him dragging his knapsack out of the barracks and getting into a German truck. Aimee and Adele, even though they hardly see the Commandant anymore, claim he hasn't mentioned Frederick's name since that day either. It is so strange and I fear the worst for him."

Nettie nodded. As she walked Clea down the path to the house, she informed her, "I won't be coming back to school again. I'm sorry. Marie-Claire will have to handle them without me. They like her more anyway."

Clea nodded sadly and began her way down the main road on her own and then turned around and walked a few paces back to Nettie. "Nett, I'll tell Marie-Claire and Mr. LaPierre that you won't be back. But then I, too, will be gone."

"What do you mean, Clea?" a concerned Nettie inquired.

"I'll tell you someday Nett. Someday. I just wanted to see you again. Goodbye." With that she turned and walked down the road.

Nettie watched her until she disappeared from view. So, Clea had to go into hiding. Another loss. Would she ever see her again? As she pulled her sweater closer around her, she walked slowly toward the farmhouse and sat on the porch steps. She also wondered about Frederick. What had happened to him? Obviously Rolfe had found out he had lied about Commandant Neumann's demise. Nettie put her face in her hands and cried. But she quickly stopped and wiped her tears away. Why would she cry for Frederick? He was the enemy after all. She got back to her feet and walked to the house.

Chapter 23

The end of May slipped quietly by. Nettie either wandered the farm and orchard or slept for hours on end in her room. In her treks through the trees she lived in the past, refusing to acknowledge the here and now. She relived playing amongst the trees and bringing in the dairy cows in the fresh crisp mornings. The hardest part was trying to remember what her father and siblings looked like. It had been so long ago that they had been together. The previous four years were suppressed in her mind. She couldn't bear to think about Terese, Frederick and certainly not Rolfe.

June arrived without notice from the woman who lived in the netherworld of her own making. A few of her friends came to visit, but finding her silent and withdrawn, left after a few minutes. Nettie didn't care, about anything. Her mother and Nana were at a loss of what to do and their own daily labor sapped any energy they had.

It was on one of those early June evenings that Nettie propped open her bedroom window before she went to sleep. For some time now she would wake up in the middle of the night and hear the drone of airplane engines overhead. She knew that they were on their way to targets far away from Blanc Fleur. As she had told the children, there was nothing worth bombing in Blanc Fleur. She was so used to the sound that she always just rolled over and went back to sleep. On that night she had just gone to bed and was starting to drift off when she heard an airplane engine overhead. Her mind ignored it and she was starting to drift off again when she heard a strange sound coming from the sky. She sat up in bed and strained her ears to try and ascertain what was the sort of swooping, swishing sound. She cautiously slid from the sheets and went to the open window. She blinked her eyes to make sure she wasn't dreaming. Outside her window, over and around the orchard, she could make out about a dozen ghostly domes slowly descending to earth. One by one they landed and she could hear snapping of branches as some of them landed on the trees. Her mother and Nana appeared at her shoulder and watched the sight of clouds of parachutes land and then being drawn into bundles and disappearing.

After a few minutes nothing could be seen or heard.

"Do you think it is the invasion?" Nettie finally spoke.

Her mother whispered back, "I don't know. It is more likely it was just a landing of the Free French to aide the Resistance fighters."

Nana speculated, "Maybe they are setting the groundwork for an invasion."

"He said they would land here," Nettie said to herself.

After several minutes of nothing else to see, they started to head back to bed when they were startled to hear large trucks coming from the direction of Blanc Fleur. Oh, not again, they all thought as they looked at each other. In the next minute they heard the now familiar pounding on the door. Nana shrugged her shoulders as if to ask what choice they had and went down the stairs to open the door. Nettie and her mother walked down a few of the steps and stopped there.

Nana opened the door and was nearly knocked over as several soldiers burst threw the open door. As they proceeded to rifle through their home and belongings, Rolfe appeared in the doorway. He barked orders to his men instructing them to leave nothing untouched. It was then that he glanced in the direction of the three women on the stairs. He did a double take when he saw Nettie standing there with her cropped hair. Sharply he ordered them out of the house and they quickly made their way down the stairs and into the drizzly, chilly air outside. They huddled together on the porch and listened helplessly to the goings-on inside. At some point a soldier approached them and held out his hand that held a book.

"Why was this hidden in the clock?" Without having to look at it, Nettie knew he was referring to her copy of "The Grapes of Wrath." She quickly spoke up and answered, "It's a first edition and valuable."

The soldier grinned and answered, "Gut." He stuck it into his pocket and turned to re-enter the house when Rolfe stopped him and ordered him to hand the book to him. Rolfe took one look at the title and author and with an angry look that caused Nettie to cringe inwardly, pitched it over the side of the porch and they heard it splash as it landed in a puddle somewhere in the dark.

Looking at Nettie's mother, he then ordered, "Go into the house and get some clothes together for each of you. You have five minutes."

"We had nothing to do with those people landing in our orchard," protested Eulalie.

Rolfe glared at her and repeated, "You have five minutes." And with that he turned on his heels and walked off the porch and went to join some soldiers who where in the process of knocking down the door to the work shed. Nettie watched in horror as they easily knocked the door off its hinges and shined their lights around the interior. Surely Rolfe had seen the hidden cupboard when he had found her with his radio. After a cursory look around the tiny building, Rolfe ordered them out and instructed one of his men to bring some gasoline from one of the trucks and soak the interior. After his instructions were carried out, he himself struck a match and flung it into the interior and the shed was instantly engulfed in flames. Rolfe continued to stand there and watch it burn while the other soldiers made their way through the orchard and

Nettie could only guess they were heading to the distillery. Would they burn that too?

Nettie's attention was drawn back to Rolfe who stood with shoulders hunched over and his arms crossed in front of him, staring into the flames. Her mother then returned with three pillowcases stuffed with clothing. She handed one to Nettie and another to Nana. She looked at the burning shed and whispered, "I wonder if they'll burn everything?"

They didn't answer, as they had already feared the same thing.

They stood there in silence as they watched the shed crumble and fall into a pile of flaming boards. It was only then that Rolfe turned around and walked back to the shivering women.

"Get into the truck," he ordered. A couple of soldiers herded the women toward a truck parked on the street and helped them into the back. Her mother and Nana sat on the bench along the interior that faced away from the house. "I can't bear to see them burn it," murmured Nana. Nettie sat across from them and scanned the orchard and house.

She wanted to look at it one more time, perhaps for the last time. A few minutes later the rest of the soldiers came back to the trucks and the engines roared to life and they jerked into gear. As the truck gathered up speed, Nettie scanned the darkness and reported to Nana, who was holding her head in her hands, "I don't see any flames other than those from the shed."

The three women together watched as the house and orchard disappeared in the darkness. The last sight they could make out was the glowing shed.

The convoy of trucks pulled in front of the small jail and the truck in which they were riding jerked to a stop, nearly throwing them out of the back of the vehicle. Soldiers appeared and helped them down.

"Take them inside," ordered Rolfe from his position next to the threshold of the main entrance to the jail. They were marched inside and ordered up the narrow stone steps that led to the upper floors. At the first landing, Nana and Eulalie were ordered to follow a pair of soldiers while

Rolfe himself ordered Nettie upward to the next floor. She went slowly, as the way was now only lit by the single flashlight held by Rolfe. She made her way to the cell he indicated and went alone inside. She watched him as he turned the key in the lock and with a nod of his head he departed. She looked through the barred, small window cut into the ancient wooden door and watched him walk away, leaving her alone in the dark. She listened to his steps as they echoed down the stone steps. It was only after silence crept in that she turned around and looked about her.

It was the same cell she had occupied when she had been brought here after Commandant Neumann had died. She placed her bundle of clothes next to the mattress that was placed in one of the corners of the small cell. She went to the barred window and looked out. A few lights could be made out here and there about the small town. Clouds blocked out the moon and as she stood there, falling raindrops splashed her. In the darkness she could make out the courtyard below her. Her mind flashed the memory of Rolfe offering the condemned man a blindfold before ordering the firing squad to do its job. Would he serve her the same kindness in the morning? As exhaustion overtook her fear, she lay down on the mattress and fell asleep.

Lacking a watch or a clock, Nettie had no idea what time it was when she finally awoke the next day. She could not see the sun as it was raining and overcast. In awhile she noticed people scurrying about the streets and could only guess they were seeking an afternoon meal. She could have called out to some people she recognized as they passed below, but fearing it could cause trouble if they tried to help her and her family, she stayed silent. It was sometime in the afternoon that she would have her only visitor. One of the soldiers made his way up to her cell and set a bowl of stew, a small loaf of bread, and a pitcher of water inside. Without a word to her he locked the door and left.

The day turned into night and she figured that at least for today, there would be no firing squad. With nothing to do, she lay down again on the mattress and fell asleep while listening to the rhythm of the rain outside.

Chapter 24

It had still been light outside when she fell asleep, but it was dark when someone grasped her shoulder and shook her awake. She opened her eyes to make out Rolfe leaning over her. His eyes stared intently into her face. She sat up and asked, "Is it time?"

He stood up and stepped back. "Get up, Nettie."

She looked at him incomprehensibly. It was then that she noticed the distant sound of thunder. She stood up and looked out the window. She noticed that it was just past dawn, but the sky was so overcast it seemed earlier. The thunder seemed to roll almost continuously. She looked up at Rolfe and spoke softly, "Could you at least wait until the storm is over?"

Rolfe, realizing what she was thinking said gently, "Nettie, the invasion has begun. You can leave."

She looked disbelieving at him and walked out the door and down the short corridor to the window at the end. Nettie looked out toward the channel. She could see soft black clouds in the morning light. She could now feel the thunder as well as hear it. She turned around and looked at Rolfe and noticed he was wearing a faded uniform that bore the rank of Oberleutnant. She reasoned it must have been the uniform from his days in the Afrika Corps.

"Where are you going?"

"I have been ordered to take what few men I have under my command and head to the beaches."

"You will fight?"

"That would be my duty, Nettie. I have come to do my final duty."

"What would that be?" she asked suddenly fearful.

He looked at the shivering woman before him and replied, "I am here to release my last prisoner. You are free to leave." He reached into his breast pocket and pulled out a key and held it out to her.

"Where are my mother and Nana?"

"They were released yesterday. Your mother came back last night and asked me to give this to you when I released you. She said you would know where it fit."

Was this a trap? She took the key from the tired shell of a man she used to know. "Why did you keep me? Why are you letting me go?"

He turned around and walked slowly to the stairs.

"Rolfe, why?" she demanded.

He turned back around and said simply, "Because you are my friend."

A flash of red-hot anger surged through her body. She clenched her fists and looked at him right in the eye as she said, "I was never your *friend*. I could never be a friend to the dog who murdered my family and my friends. I have *hated* you! I have always *hated* you! Now tuck your tail between your legs and run back to your country. I never want to see you or your kind ever again!" Even Nettie herself was surprised at the venom in her voice.

He merely stood looking at her before he spoke. "I am not running away Nettie, I am going to the beaches. May you get your wish, Nettie, and never see me again. Good-bye." And with that he turned back around and hurried down the hall and down the stairs.

For a minute Nettie just stood there, listening to the sounds of the invasion, the sound of advancing freedom! The percussion of the artillery and bombs was so powerful that she could feel the vibrations through her bare feet on the stone floor. Suddenly she sprang into action, gathered up her few items of clothing and put them in the pillowcase her mother had used as a suitcase a few days before. She didn't need to dress as she had slept in old workpants and shirt because she had feared that she would be dragged before the firing squad in her nightgown. She tiptoed down the stone steps to the first landing heading down the center of the cells of that floor. They were all empty. She went down the steps at the other end of the second floor to the main floor. It was empty. Not a single soldier was to be seen. The rooms were in shambles. Papers were strewn all around; file drawers were open and emptied of their contents. She took a detour down a narrow corridor and opened the door to the large room that had been used as the courtroom at her so-called trial the summer before. Why she wanted to see it again, she wasn't sure. It too, was devoid of life. A few tables and chairs were stacked in a corner and these file cabinets were ransacked as well. The Germans had obviously tried to wipe away any evidence of their crimes and activities. But she would remember; they would *all* remember.

Opening the door to the street, Nettie found the inhabitants of Blanc Fleur running here and there in the streets. She slipped out and held her few remaining items she owned to her chest. A few of the people she recognized were from outlying farms, frightened by the fighting on the beaches and seeking refuge in the town or were trying to reach safe areas further inland. Mixed in with the people were an array of farm animals that were being driven by their owners or had broken out of their fields and were fleeing the never-ending thunder. Nettie carefully made her way down the street, trying to avoid being run over by humans and animals alike. She stopped a few people she knew and asked for news of the invasion. All she was able to ascertain was that it had started that morning just before dawn and it seemed to be both an air and sea assault. No one knew if it was successful as of yet.

Nettie stepped into a doorway and pulled the key out of her pocket. It was an ancient key. In what door would it fit? Would they have gone to Aunt Elita's? Or perhaps to the Farve house. No, Nettie reasoned to herself. If it had been to a private home, why wouldn't they just tell Rolfe? Why didn't they go home? She looked at the key again and realized that it had been given to Rolfe *before* the invasion. It must therefore be a place she could go to and be hidden from the Germans if they came for her again after releasing her. How did they know he would be releasing her? So many questions! After a few minutes of thinking in the quiet doorway, an idea came to her. She walked quickly to the nearest corner and turned. Down that street she came to the library. It looked deserted. She waited until no one was in sight and she took the key and put it into the lock and it turned. The door came right open and she quickly shut the old door behind her. She stood alone in the dark. She shouted a greeting and her voice echoed about the interior. She sighed as she sat down at a study table. Where had they gone? Had Rolfe lied and never released them? Had they given up on her coming to join them? Perhaps they had rushed to the farm when the bombing had started. She laid her head on her arms and shut her eyes, thinking of what she should do next.

"I wondered who was here," said a voice from behind her. Nettie jumped; startled that she had not heard a sound. It was Lily. "We were waiting for you Nett, come with me."

Nettie followed her to the back of the library where Lily knelt down and pushed against a slab of stone that recessed several inches before she was able to push it to the side. Revealed was a small opening of about two feet wide and three feet high.

Lily motioned for Nettie to go first. "There are stairs leading down, they are very steep so be careful," Lily warned. There was a soft glow emanating from somewhere far below, but even so, Nettie was forced to make her way inch by inch down the narrow, slippery steps that were carved from the rock on which the library sat. After a few harrowing moments, Nettie was standing at the bottom of the steps. Her eyes strained to grow accustomed to the dim light.

"Nettie!" called several voices a few feet from her. She blinked her eyes and could make out her mother and Nana sitting against a wall. She squealed in delight and threw herself in their open arms. It was after she greeted her mother and Nana that she became aware of all the other people sitting or laying around them. One woman came out of the dark and threw her arms around Nettie and gave her a bear hug. Clea! Nettie was so pleased to see her friend again. "I thought you had to leave Blanc Fleur," was all Nettie could think to say in her surprise.

Clea laughed and clapped her hands in obvious glee at seeing Nettie again. "I did leave Blanc Fleur. I came here, to the underworld, the day after I saw you. I expected to leave France soon after, but things were happening and I was told to just stay put. Now I know why."

Nettie, still somewhat in a haze over the events of the past few days just looked blankly at her friend.

"Come and sit down," said Clea, "and I will start from the beginning."

"Please do," replied Nettie as they sat down on one of the many cushions lying around the floor.

Clea cocked her head in deep thought and after a moment she began. "Well, as you have probably already guessed, I have my ties to the Resistance movement. I have been hiding downed soldiers and others down here for years. This is where the Colliers came with the Klein sisters and this is where your friend Jacques came after he fled your orchard."

"How did you find out about this place? And what *is* this place?"

"This was originally just the cellar that the priests and nuns used to store their food centuries ago when this building was a church. When St. Mary's Church was built it was put to different uses until it became a library. Somewhere along the way the entrance was made to what it is today. It was Lily who came across some old writings of the history of Blanc Fleur that mentioned hiding Huguenots in the old church cellar until they could be smuggled to England. She searched for some time before finding it. This was years ago and she kept it to herself, always thinking it might come in handy some day. I guess that day has come!"

"But how did you find out?"

"I went around town and started asking rather oblique questions about the Germans, the war, what their feelings were. After awhile I zeroed in on a few people and asked a few more questions. Gradually Lily asked me a few oblique questions and somehow we got around to the fact I had people to hide and she had a place to hide them."

"Who else knew?"

"Just Lily and I, Father Bolet...and Frederick."

"Frederick?"

"Yes, Frederick. You see Nett, I had met Frederick years ago, in Germany. You have met my Aunt Marie-Christine." Nettie nodded. Clea continued, "She is a professor of religion in Paris. Her specialty is researching various Christian sects and several years ago she went to Berlin to meet with several members of the Society of Friends, or Quakers as they are sometimes called. She took me with her for company and one of the families we met with was the Von Allmon family. The couple and their three girls and the youngest, a boy."

"Frederick," Nettie finished.

"Yes," confirmed Clea. It had been years since I had seen him, but I remembered the name and well, that hair was hard to forget." Clea looked thoughtful. "I wish I knew where he was."

"Was he the one who told you to go into hiding?"

"Well, I would say no."

Nettie looked quizzically at her and Clea went on to explain. "I was in my classroom when Rolfe knocked on the door and handed me a note saying it was from Frederick. It said that it was no longer safe and

I needed to go into hiding. Of course I know it wasn't from Frederick at all."

"How do you know?"

"He never sent me notes, he always came in person. The handwriting wasn't his and I doubt if an aide would have his boss deliver a message for him."

"Do you think it was Rolfe?" asked Nettie.

"Yes, I do. I wasn't sure if it was a trick or not, but I decided I couldn't take a chance that it wasn't. I knew from Frederick that Rolfe was under pressure from his superiors to put an end to the Resistance activities in the area."

"I take it there was a lot going on," commented Nettie.

Clea threw her head back and laughed, "Oh yes. There was so much going on. Actually there was plenty going on in your own back yard."

"What do you mean?" asked Nettie as her mother and Nana drew closer as to hear this part of the conversation.

"Your orchard was a perfect landmark to use for incoming Allied spies and Resistance people for one thing."

"Why?"

Her mother spoke up and asked, "Nettie, think about the wells and cisterns. What shape do they form?"

Nettie thought for a minute before exclaiming "An X! They make an X."

"Yep," confirmed Clea. "As they say, X marks the spot! And the wide road in back of your farm was used as a landing strip for small planes."

Nana spoke up then. "That is what it was used for during the Great War."

Nettie looked confused. "It was a landing strip? Why don't I remember that?"

Her mother interjected with, "You were so young, and we kept you away from there, and…other things were happening in our lives. It was actually a landing strip before the war, as your father's brothers would fly in from Alsace for visits. After the war it was just used as a back road for the farmers whose land backed up to it."

Nettie searched her memory, but could not bring back anything concerning airplanes that would have been virtually in her backyard.

Lily walked over to the small group and said, "Sorry, but you need to extinguish the lantern. We don't know how much longer we will be down here."

They turned the flame down until it left them in total blackness. Nettie leaned against the damp wall and spoke in Clea's direction. "Is this how you have lived for the last few weeks?""

Out of the darkness she answered, "Only part of the time, I was able to slip upstairs when the library was closed. The walls are so thick that no one could hear me. The hardest part was not having anyone to talk to most of the time."

"Now you're making up for it," teased Nettie.

"You're a captive audience," Clea replied.

Nettie answered with, "Tell me everything, I have a feeling we have the time."

And so Clea launched into a long oration of the activities in which she had participated over the last four years.

Nettie couldn't resist asking about her disappearance during the Christmas pageant.

"Oh that," dismissed Clea. "I took a few members of the Resistance to the landing strip behind your orchard and a plane landed for a few minutes and then took them to England. It was a great opportunity since everyone was here in town."

"Clea, you could have just opted out of the play, why the deception with Adele taking your place?"

"Our dear Commandant was onto me. I knew that if something went wrong I needed an alibi that even he couldn't deny. I needed to buy time to continue the work of helping the Underground. I guess I will always wonder to my dying day why the Commandant has done what he has done. I doubt if he or Frederick will see the end of this day."

In the dark Nettie shivered. Where was Rolfe? Frederick? But she tried to push the thought of them from her mind. She shouldn't, no, she wouldn't care.

"So, Nett, I have babbled on long enough, what happened when he came to release you? Your mother said he released them yesterday and told them to stay in town, near you."

She lowered her voice and whispered, "They were fearing the worst when he said that. They went to my mother's house and my mother talked to Lily and arranged to have you hidden down here in case you were released. We figured we could smuggle you out with me. Your mother took a key to the Commandant, just in case she or Nana weren't in town to help you. They didn't think it would be safe for you to return to the farm. So, what did he say when he let you go?"

For the first time the wave of realization of what Rolfe had done for her and indeed, her family and Clea, hit her. She also remembered what she had said to him in parting. "He said nothing. Nothing." She mumbled as she laid down, suddenly feeling exhausted, as the emotions of the last four years seemed to slam into her at once. They lapsed into silence and listened to what they had hoped and prayed for the last four years advance toward them.

Chapter 25

For the next several days they stayed hidden in their basement cave beneath the library. Occasionally they would venture up the narrow stairs and make their way to the privy in the yard behind the library. Normally they would have taken the opportunity to breathe fresh air, but they found they were merely exchanging stale, damp air for air filled with smoke and debris. The thunder from the beaches stopped on the first day, but it was replaced by the sporadic thunder coming from various directions as the Allied bombers took out the railways, bridges, and roads leading to the coast. Since Blanc Fleur lacked any strategic targets, they felt safe from any air raids. However, since the road from the beaches led into Blanc Fleur and then on to several larger towns, they feared the Germans would be retreating through their town. What retreating Germans would do in retaliation concerned them all.

Not only did they need to stay out of sight of any Germans, but also of fellow townsmen. They didn't have room for any more people in the basement and they also knew that while they were out of sight for now, if they were discovered they would be cornered. Several times while they were hidden below in the dark, they would hear the sounds of feet and voices overhead. They couldn't be sure if they were civilians seeking cover or Germans searching the buildings for Allied soldiers. During those times they stayed as still as possible, barely able to breathe until the noises stopped.

On what would prove to be the fourth morning, Lily ventured up the narrow stairs and out the tiny doorway. She was gone for what seemed like an hour and several began to voice their concern about her safety. Suddenly, they heard what seemed like hundreds of footsteps overhead and the tiny doorway was opened up. A large form was squeezing itself through the narrow opening and then proceeded to slide the rest of the way down the stairs, landing at the bottom with an 'Oomph!' at Nettie's feet. She gasped when she recognized Mr. LaPierre.

He looked up at her and shouted, "It's over! The Allies are marching through Blanc Fleur as we speak!"

Cheers and exclamations of disbelief filled the hollow room. As if on cue, everyone scrambled for the stairs at once, nearly trampling the still-seated Mr. LaPierre. Nettie was one of the first up the stairs and into the library that was full of townspeople trying to avoid the crush of the people in the streets. Nettie elbowed her way out the door and stared at the sight of Allied trucks and tanks rolling by. Horns blared, bells rang and people were shouting and throwing confetti from the rooftops. Her mother and Nana joined her and they watched for a few minutes before Clea said she wished to check on the rest of the town. Nettie said she would join her and together they elbowed their way down the street.

"Come on up here girls!" came a voice beside them. They looked up to find a group of British soldiers astride a tank. Several held out their hands and they gratefully accepted the ride. For some time they rode around picking up other girls and young boys who helped themselves to a seat. Nettie was relieved to see that the town seemed untouched except for some pock marks in the sides of buildings and a few burned homes and shops. The burly soldier that kept his arm around her to keep her from falling off explained that they had met with little resistance in the town but had run into a pocket of Germans just outside of town. Nettie couldn't help but wonder if one of them had been Rolfe. As they turned a corner, Nettie looked the opposite direction and could make out a sea of humanity at the end of the street.

"What is that?" she asked the soldier.

"I think it's the soldiers we captured on our way in. Looks like your people are having a shot at them now."

"Let me down." she requested, suddenly devoid of any festive spirit.

"What?" the soldier asked.

"Please, I must get down." She wriggled out of his protective arms and landed on the street. She looked up to catch Clea's words "I hope you find him, Nett," before the tank picked up speed and left her behind. She turned and with her heart in her throat, made her way as quickly as possible to the large throng of people who were cursing and throwing anything they could get their hands on, mostly decaying vegetables and stones. The target of their hatred was a group of about thirty German soldiers who were being guarded by several Canadian soldiers who half-heartedly tried to quell the hostility. Nettie searched the features of each soldier over carefully. They were each filthy and mud covered from the several days of fighting. She did not see either Rolfe or Frederick amongst them. A sense of dread came over her. Surely there were other German captives in the area, there had been thousands stationed in the area. A hand at her elbow turned her around and she came face to face with Anna.

Anna related an amazing tale of her and her family weathering the invasion in their root cellar and eventually being evacuated to the town by the advancing forces. There were snipers all around and it was not safe for them to stay.

"Have you heard about our farm?" asked Nettie.

Anna hesitated before saying, "I can't swear that it is your farm and my English is not very good, as you know. Some of the soldiers were talking about an airplane that landed on a house and took off the second story. I think it may have been your house, Nett, but I'm not sure."

Nettie nodded numbly. She knew it was much too dangerous to even attempt to leave Blanc Fleur at the moment and she dreaded telling her mother and Nana that their home might not be there when they could return.

"I heard all of you had been arrested; did the Brits release you?"

Nettie shook her head, "No, Rolfe released us before he left for the beaches. Have you seen him Anna?"

"No. You don't suppose they would just execute him on sight do you?"

It was a question Nettie had wondered about herself. "When I saw him last he was wearing the uniform that he had worn in North Africa; maybe that would hide his identity," was all she could guess. She left Anna and made her way down the packed street. She came across several Canadian soldiers standing and sitting on a stoop and asked in her broken English where German prisoners may be found. One of the men reached into a pocket and handed her something. It was wrapped in dark brown paper and had the words *HERSHEY* emblazoned across it. She took a deep whiff and discovered it was chocolate. She thanked the soldier and he spoke. "A few krauts are being held for questioning at your jail before being shipped out…" He hadn't finished the sentence before the small French woman ran off in the direction of the jail. "Hit a few of them krauts for me, sister," he yelled as the others laughed.

She didn't know why she was going there. What was she going to do or say to him if he happened to be there anyway? She stopped and stood on the sidewalk facing the jail. Allied soldiers were to be seen coming and going from the building; should she go closer? A quote from Dostoevsky flashed in her mind, it went something like "Much unhappiness has come into the world…because…of things left unsaid." She had to try, had to see if he was here.

Clenching her fists she walked determinedly toward the building. Before she reached her destination, she heard voices from the courtyard and changed her course and went around to the back. The main gate was opened to allow a small truck to back up into the small yard. Allied soldiers were everywhere and for a minute Nettie thought the prisoners might have already left. She decided to loiter, trying to pick up the English words flying back and forth between the men. She was able to understand that several officers were still inside. No one paid any attention to the short, scruffy woman waiting around by the back gate, so Nettie wasn't forced to make up any stories of why she was hanging about. Occasionally she would stroll around to the front of the jail to ensure that she didn't miss any thing. On one of her strolls she noticed soldiers building a bonfire of the trash and odds and ends that the Germans had left behind. She stood idly in the background while one poured gasoline on the pile of junk and another flung a lit match. A shot of orange flame sprang up and within seconds the pile was engulfed. Nettie then turned and was heading back toward the courtyard when something made her stop and turn back around when she heard a soldier shout, "Hey! Let's throw this piece of Nazi junk in there!" She watched as the soldier raised his arms and flung something on top of the flaming pile. The object was quickly ablaze, but Nettie could easily see that it was a small radio. A small silver and mahogany radio. She bit her lip and headed toward the back of the building to wait.

After a half-hour wait, Nettie heard shouting from inside the jail and the back door opened up. In single file, about twenty men shuffled the short distance from the door to the truck where they climbed into the back of the covered transport vehicle. Nettie stared hard at each of the men. She saw the end of the line and had not recognized any of them. She found a lump growing in her throat and she swallowed hard. Wait! She looked again at the man who was next to last in the line. Could it be? She was afraid of the disappointment if it was not he. But it was. She first noticed that his dark blonde hair appeared a reddish brown and she realized with horror that the color was from dried blood mixed into his hair. His clothes were dirty and torn and he wore the coat of a private that must have been two sizes bigger than him. His head was down and he did not look to the side as he climbed into the back of the truck and the low tailgate was raised. She was afraid of attracting attention to herself and waited where she stood. The truck started up and as it slowly made its way out of the yard and just cleared the gate, the engine stalled. Nettie took advantage of the few extra seconds to fly the few steps to the back of the truck and look inside. He was sitting on the near bench and she reached toward him. She wanted to touch the weary face that was covered in dirt and dried blood. His aquiline nose appeared to have been broken and a long cut jagged across his forehead. Her hand would only reach to his knee, where she gently laid her hand. His gray eyes lifted and looked deeply into hers. Part of her wanted to be happy to see this man so broken, but instead she found her heart breaking.

She whispered, "Good-bye, Mein freunden."

He clasped her hand in his swollen, cut hands and squeezed them tightly. Only the forward motion of the truck reluctantly separated the two. Their eyes were locked on each other as the truck pulled forward and turned a corner. Nettie stayed where she stood for several long moments, oblivious to the curious soldiers glancing her way. When she did move, it was with a slight smile. She headed back to the library to tell her mother and Nana what she had discovered about the fate of their home and that their town was still standing. She would tell them she had found Rolfe, but the details would remain buried in her heart.

Several days later found Nettie with broom in hand ready to clean out the schoolroom she shared with Marie-Claire. The building was still standing and basically unscathed, but soldiers from both sides and civilians had used it to hide or live during those anxious days. The building across the courtyard that had been the German Headquarters was now occupied by Allied troops and still off limits to the residents of Blanc Fleur.

"You know you will have your own class again, as soon as the troops move eastward," stated Marie-Claire.

"Yes, I know and I am counting the days!" enthused Nettie as she swept up a pile of ripped papers. She sobered for a minute and continued, "But it will be different. Nothing will be as before. If you know what I mean."

They were both thinking of the conversation they had overheard while passing a group of French Canadian soldiers. They had been talking about how lucky the residents of Blanc Fleur were. Curious, the two women had stopped and chatted with them. It was then that they learned the extent of the horrors of the invasion and subsequent fighting that they had either guessed or heard rumors. The battle of the beaches close to Blanc Fleur, which the soldiers referred to by the rather peculiar name of "Omaha", had been the fiercest of all of the areas invaded that day. Men had drowned or been shot before even hitting the beach. The hedgerows or what the locals call boscages had hidden German snipers that were firing at the Allied troops. But what sent chills up both of their backs was the tale relayed by one of the soldiers. "A buddy of mine told me that when they marched into Oradour-Sur-Glane a couple days ago, all they found was a smoldering church. You know what was inside? Over six hundred men, women and children. Only two, a woman and a young boy escaped. I guess the krauts were upset that the civilians attacked a convoy heading to the coast. Big threat to them krauts, I guess. Saw a lot of dead animals and civilians and burned buildings myself. You're lucky your Commandant just burned his files and not the town. You know it was my unit that captured him up near the beaches."

"Really? Commandant Wieber?" inquired Marie-Claire.

"Yep. Of course we didn't know who he was at the time. One of the other krauts turned him in thinking he would be rewarded. He wasn't. But we interrogated your ex-commandant and found him just a low ranking officer and since the town was still standing, we just shipped him off with the other captives."

The two women continued to listen to the soldiers for some time before excusing themselves, then made their way to the school building to join the others cleaning up the classroom in anticipation of beginning school in a week or two.

Marie-Claire nodded and replied, "I have prayed about it for the last week and later I am going to talk to Mother about going to Germany when the war is actually over."

"I will miss you," answered Nettie.

"I haven't left yet!" laughed Marie-Claire. "Besides I do plan to return someday. Did I tell you my family is coming next month?"

"Really? From Rennes?"

Marie-Claire nodded, smiling. "Of course I had a few visits from Momma and Pere the last few years, but they were afraid to bring Josie, Rosa, and Philippe with them. They must be so big now! I wonder if I will recognize them?" she mused.

"I am sure you will," assured Nettie. "Lets hurry, I'm anxious to finish and have everyone meet at the café for the last bottle of 'Dupre's Finest.'"

"Well, I hope it's not the *last* bottle!" commented Marie-Claire.

Nettie shrugged and replied, "I guess that will be answered when we can go home and see the place for ourselves." She changed the subject by asking if Marie-Claire had seen Clea in the last day or two. The young nun shook her head. "I haven't seen her since she came back from her trip to the beaches. She was so distressed by what she saw that she did mention that she wanted some time to herself, but she was planning on being at the café this afternoon."

"Did they bury Frederick's body in the Farve family plot?"

"Yes. Although it took a direct order from a General to let her have the body and bury him in a French cemetery. I understand they told her just to throw it in a ditch with all the others. The priest who buried him said they could only bury him if they agreed to bury him in the middle of the night and no one but Clea and her mother were allowed to attend."

"Has his family been notified?"

"Not that I know of. It will be years before everything will be straightened out."

"I know," murmured Nettie, thinking of her own sister in her own unmarked grave far away.

At that minute they heard a voice calling from the courtyard "Nettie! Nettie are you there?"

"Sounds like Clea," said Marie-Claire as she went to the open window and looked out.

She leaned out the window and answered that Nettie was indeed present.

"Tell her to come down," was Clea's shouted reply.

Marie-Claire retracted her body from the open window and stood up. "She wants you to come down. She has some man with her."

"Some man? Oh not another one! Let me look from here." She moved to the open window and looked out. She looked hard at the dark haired man standing two floors beneath her. After a second she screamed and gave a "whoop" before running out of the room and down the stairs. She hit the cobblestones at a dead run and jumped into the waiting arms of Pierre, her brother.

She hung onto him for several minutes before she loosened her hold on him. He held her at arms length and looked at her. "Nett! You look so…different."

"Four years and a war will do that," she tried to tease before she burst into tears. "I have so much to tell you, Pierre."

"I know. Clea already told me some of what I missed. The rest can wait awhile. I wanted to tell you that I have been to the farm and I am happy to report that while the house is damaged we should be able to live in it. The distillery is still standing and some trees were damaged, but most are still standing."

Nettie smiled at the wonderful news and her brother went on, "I would like to come home Nett, that is, if that is OK with you, Mother, and Nana."

His older sister burst into tears anew and she embraced him and whispered into his ear, "You can come back only if you promise never to go away again."

He hugged her hard and replied that once the Germans were pushed out of France he would gladly promise never to leave again. Then he said, "I have someone for you to meet."

"Really? Who might that be?"

He turned around and for the first time Nettie saw a young woman standing quietly behind them. "This is my wife, Evelyn."

Nettie smiled and held out her hand. "Welcome to the family."

Chapter 26

Nettie awakened from her deep thoughts of the past. She looked out the window and sighed. The Dupres had come home a few days after their reunion with Pierre and started to repair the damage to their house. They had been thankful that the house had not caught fire and burned to the ground. For over a year the five of them had lived on what had been their first floor while their energies had been directed at building a home near the distillery for Pierre and his wife and refurbishing the stills and re-entering the Calvados brandy business. A few trees had been crushed by the advancing troops and even today when they cut down trees they would often find shrapnel and bullets imbedded in the wood. The effects of the war were felt for years, both financially and personally. A few weeks after Paris was liberated Adele had gone to the fields to bring in the dairy cows. When the cows came home without her, Anna had gone out to look for her and discovered her body in a field. She had stepped on a land mine that had been discarded by one of the armies during the fighting.

She picked up the empty bottle of "Dupre's Finest" that sat on her dresser. The neck had been cut off and sanded down. It now was used to hold her spare change. She well remembered sitting at the café with her brother and colleagues and drinking a few drops of the brandy. Marie-Claire had been right, it wasn't the last bottle of Calvados ever produced, but it was the last produced in that innocent time before the war, before everything. Pierre had done a fine job restarting the business and Nettie had let him be in charge of that end of the business and she had taken over the running of the orchard itself, and as things improved financially she had even bought back the land behind the orchard and ran a small dairy.

She placed the bottle back on the dresser and gently picked up the tiny glass house that also sat on her dresser. The paint was flaking off the red door and blue shutters and the red ribbon was faded and worn, but Nettie treasured the ornament. She had found it in a box of Christmas decorations that had been placed in Pierre's bedroom. After the airplane had shorn off the top floor of the house, exposing the contents of the upper floor, not much could be salvaged. She had taken one look at the box of glass shards and nearly tossed the entire contents when she happened to see the intact roof of the miniature house. She had gingerly reached into the box and pulled on the ribbon, lifting it out of the surrounding debris. "Protection," she had said to herself as she had cupped it in her hand while throwing the rest of the box on the junk heap. Protection, that was what the little house had signified and indeed, she had had that. She could see that now. Ever since that day the little house had sat on her dresser, except when she placed it amongst the greens over the fireplace during the Christmas season.

Reluctantly she had placed the house next to the bottle and took a deep breath. For some reason she rather dreaded reading the letter. She had kept those memories buried for so long. Right after the war she had told her friends the details of what had happened to Commandant Neumann and the role Frederick had played. She told them about the radio and the shooting in the orchard that resulted in the death of Father Bolet. She had told them everything that had happened, that is everything except saying good-bye to him and how she had felt. Some things were meant to stay in one's heart.

Nettie finally turned her attention back to the letter on her lap. She smoothed the folded sheets and smiled when she still recognized the neat handwriting on the pages. She took another deep breath and began to read the words before her.

My Dearest Nettie:

How does one reach across fifteen years? I have started this letter several times as I don't know where to begin to tell you all that I want to. I guess in that case, I shall start at the very beginning and try to remember as I go along.

It was not an accident that I came to Blanc Fleur. While I was but a low-ranking officer in North Africa, I had connections, as I think I told you that my family were neighbors and were friendly with the Rommel family. After pulling out of North Africa and waiting for my next assignment, I expressed my desire to return to France to Herr Rommel. Hearing about the trial and the need for a new commandant, he pulled strings and had me assigned there with the direct order of ascertaining the truth of what had happened. I did indeed attend your (and Frederick's) trial. What you probably don't know is that Frederick had told the officials that he suspected that you were either the head or part of a large ring of subversives. You were seen as more valuable alive than dead. However, it became clear rather quickly that you weren't part of any group engaged in that activity and the demise of the previous commandant was not a part of any plot. It was not until the end I discovered that Clea was the person I was looking for all that time.

Nettie paused at those words. She had to laugh now, as it was only after the war that it was learned of the considerable activities of the underground in the area and of Clea's very active role. Who knew the beautiful blonde could be so pretty and devious? Nettie had just heard from Clea just the week before. She had written that she, her American husband and six children where doing well and that she loved Los

Angeles. She had invited Nettie to visit and told her of the wonderful fruit trees she had in her very own back yard. Her own orange trees—imagine!

The last few months at Blanc Fleur were the most difficult of my life. I made the mistake of getting to know the people of the area. I felt more at home there than I did with my own countrymen. I no longer cared about the war; I was horrified by what had happened, what was still happening all in the name of Germany. I decided to befriend the citizens of Blanc Fleur and turn a blind eye to what I knew was going on around me. I naively hoped that the activity would stop and we could all get through the war together. I honestly don't know what was more terrifying, being in the position of such power or in the position of powerlessness that I soon found myself.

My plans began to unravel when Herr Rommel came to visit me after he had assumed command of Northern France. He had heard stories of the activities going on in my area and was questioning my effectiveness and devotion to the Fatherland. That hurt me as he was a man I much loved and respected and worst of all he was right. He sent some of the elite troops (the SS) to 'help' me you could say. I knew the war was coming to some sort of closing by that point, but I knew I was losing control and if I lost control then not only would I face the firing squad, but the civilians could face retaliation as well. We had a tip about the priest and it was him we were following when we came to your orchard that night. You will never know the horror when you ran into me that night. I didn't know what to do, except to keep you quiet and out of the way. I came to talk to you about it when I found you working on my radio. It confirmed my hunch that Frederick was involved in some kind of illegal activity. I was so angry with you! I wanted to protect you. You and the other residents of Blanc Fleur, but no one would stop the activities and I couldn't protect everyone unless they did. After I left you, I had to confront Frederick before the SS might think of questioning him. To his credit he never admitted anything, gave no one away, but I knew he had to leave and quickly. I arranged to have him transferred to the beach where I found out several years ago that he died during the invasion. I wish I could express my sorrow at the loss...

Frederick! Nettie smiled softly as she thought of the redheaded young man. She already knew his fate as Clea had identified his body and had him buried in an unmarked grave in the Farve family plot. A year after the war, about the same time as the body of her sister had been brought back to Blanc Fleur, Frederick's remains had been returned to his native Berlin.

After the war I was able to track down an acquaintance from the beach that had arranged for Frederick to be stationed there, a Herr Muhlenberg. He told me the following story that he had heard from a soldier in Frederick's unit. Frederick was assigned to a bunker at what is now called Omaha Beach, in the same area as we spent so many pleasant times. When the invasion began he was ordered to start firing at the enemy below. He refused. He simply put his rifle down and sat in a corner of the bunker and took a Bible out of his pocket and began to read. The officer in charge ordered him to take his position. which he refused to do. They were too preoccupied to do anything at that time, not that it mattered because Frederick was shot during the battle. A few years ago, I contacted his family and tried to apologize for my actions. They told me about his association with the Society of Friends and they said they forgave me and told me Frederick had always spoken highly of me. I can't begin to say how much that means to me.

I have wondered what became of all of the inhabitants of Blanc Fleur in the last fifteen years. You, Clea, Anna, Adele, Aimee...

Nettie mentally ticked off the people mentioned in his letter. Clea was in Los Angeles, Anna and Margarethe were still teaching at the school although Nettie had given it up to devote her time to the family business. Adele of course had been gone for nearly fifteen years now. Chat and Francois were now retired and still lived in town. Mr. LaPierre had just died that spring. Lily was still the librarian and her son Dom was now teaching at the school. Aunt Elita had remarried to a local farmer and Aimee had married a businessman and moved to the south of France. The last people listed were Nana who had died several years ago and Sister Marie-Claire who had indeed gone to Germany and helped rebuild its schools. She had returned three years ago and had resumed teaching at the school.

I was taken prisoner before reaching the cliffs and after one of my own men identified me as the local commandant, I was taken to the jail with other officers and questioned. After we parted, I was taken by ship to America and then placed on a train that seemed to go on for days. I found myself in a place called Raymond, Mississippi. I spent nearly a year fighting mosquitoes, cockroaches, and snakes. If it wasn't hot and muggy it was cold and damp. But I was happy to be alive and away from the battles I heard about.

I was released in 1945 and I made my way back to Germany. I found my wife, children and parents alive and mostly well. We settled in Koln and in 1947 my wife gave birth to a baby girl. She wasn't breathing and the doctor slapped her and her eyes flew open and gave everyone in the room such an angry look. When they asked me what her name would be I found myself saying "Bernadette" since she reminded me of you. Today she is thirteen and wants to meet the "other Bernadette" that she was named for.

I would like to come to Blanc Fleur with my family. I don't want to come now when all of the planned festivities are to take place, I would like to come when it would be more quiet...

"Nettie! Are you coming down?" called Nettie's anxious mother from the bottom of the stairs.

"I'll be right there," Nettie answered. She put the letter on the dresser and knew that she would answer him right after dinner and tell him that she would welcome his visit.

And, in the fall, he came.

About the Author

Kelly Kathryn Griffin was born and raised in Flint, Michigan. She obtained her undergraduate degree in Biology at Hope College in Holland, Michigan and received her Masters in Library Sciences at Kent State University in Kent, Ohio. This book combines her love travel with that of history.

9 780595 180820